Following redundancy from her position as an IT Manager in March 2018, the author followed two dreams. Firstly, to become a published author and secondly, a personal development coach. Her varied and challenging journey, post-redundancy, gave her the courage to strive towards her dreams. Initially, she wrote for herself to help make sense of her world. However, it was always her hope to show how a highly sensitive child experiences life through the characters in her stories. 15–20% of the population have this trait, including the author and some of her children.

This book is dedicated to Graeme, my husband and my best friend. You have believed in me and supported my journey and my creativity and you know I can, even when I am in doubt. You have been swept up in the emotion I injected into the journey of my characters and even helped me name them.

Without you, I may still be hovering over the 'submit' button.

This is dedicated to my four children: Luke, Sam, Alicia and Archie, whom I am extremely proud of and who provide me with inspiration every day. They never cease to amaze me.

Nicola McDonald

In Search of the Christmas Spirit

AUSTIN MACAULEY PUBLISHERS™
LONDON • CAMBRIDGE • NEW YORK • SHARJAH

Copyright © Nicola McDonald (2020)

The right of Nicola McDonald to be identified as author of this work has been asserted by the author in accordance with section 77 and 78 of the Copyright, Designs and Patents Act 1988.

All rights reserved. No part of this publication may be reproduced, stored in a retrieval system, or transmitted in any form or by any means, electronic, mechanical, photocopying, recording, or otherwise, without the prior permission of the publishers.

Any person who commits any unauthorised act in relation to this publication may be liable to criminal prosecution and civil claims for damages.

This is a work of fiction. Names, characters, businesses, places, events, locales, and incidents are either the products of the author's imagination or used in a fictitious manner. Any resemblance to actual persons, living or dead, or actual events is purely coincidental.

A CIP catalogue record for this title is available from the British Library.

ISBN 9781528981217 (Paperback)
ISBN 9781528981224 (ePub e-book)

www.austinmacauley.com

First Published (2020)
Austin Macauley Publishers Ltd
25 Canada Square
Canary Wharf
London
E14 5LQ

Without my sister, Bernadette, I would have not heard about high sensitivity and, therefore, not have taken steps toward research and understanding.

Without the research of Elaine N. Aron, Ph.D and her book, *The Highly Sensitive Person*, and Ted Zeff's book, *The Strong Sensitive Boy*, I would still be wondering, fumbling in the dark.

Without Barbara Allen-Williams, I would not have understood my son's trait and therefore, myself less.

Belonging to a club of 15–20% of the population gives me comfort and I grew in to myself with knowledge and he grows as himself with knowledge.

Without my coach and friend, Nina Khoo, I may still be on the bottom rung. She held the ladder steady so that I could step up towards my dreams.

Without the praise of my brother, Matt, who remained so engaged, consumed by my story, I may not have believed I could move mountains.

Without Asa, the journey would have taken longer. It was our weekly sessions while striving for our PDC qualification that kept me on track and motivated.

Thank you, Sarah, for branding me 'your hero', high praise indeed from an inspirational woman.

Thank you to Adrienn and Georgina for your support and words of encouragement.

Thank you very much to Charlie Joseph, my friend and the illustrator of the front cover.

Thank you to my friends who are always there even though I'm not the best at staying in touch.

Thanks to Redundancy for opening the door to a new beginning, making way for me to pursue my passion.

Thank you to my ex-colleagues; our journey was tough but none of it wasted.

Thank you to Austin Macauley Publishers for high praise and believing in me.

In loving memory of:

Tina, thank you for giving birth to the man who became my husband and for gifting him the ability to appreciate creativity such as yours. I hope one day he'll use his. I know wherever you are now you will be proud of him; you were truly loved.

Mum, my biggest regret is that you will never see this in print, never get the chance to read it. I always want to phone you. Hope wherever you are, you know we always love you and wish we had had longer. Beyond my imagination, I don't know what is out there, but I hope you hear me, my Northern Star.

12th December 18:30 Aoife

It was dinnertime and Mummy had put Daddy's dinner on the table. It was his favourite: chicken with mashed potatoes and gravy. Daddy hated vegetables.

They all ate in silence, Mummy staring at Daddy's empty chair, her blue eyes upside down and her lips drooping towards sad.

Aoife and her little brother Aubrey just stared at each other. Aubrey pulled faces trying to make Aoife laugh. He was the cutest three-and-a-half-year-old that Aoife knew. His curly, strawberry-blond hair made him look like an angel, but he wasn't. *Anyways,* Aoife thought, *this wasn't a time for laughing,* so she kept her straight face. When Aubrey struggled to cut his food, Aoife leaned across the table and tried her best to help him, but she knocked his chicken onto the table and dripping on to the floor was the gravy.

Aubrey laughed so hard that his food catapulted from his mouth across the table into Aoife's face. "Yuck!" Aoife screamed and then quickly, "Shhh, Aubrey." By this time, Mummy had pulled herself out of her trance.

Looking at the mess, Mummy stood up in complete silence throwing Aoife her crossest look as she headed towards the kitchen. When she returned, she stretched her arm towards Aoife, handed her a damp cloth and said, "Clean it up, please."

At that same moment, Mummy's phone rang and in less time than it took for Aoife to wipe the table, Mummy said, "Fine, your dinner's in the dog," and the room fell silent again except for the echoing sound of Mummy's clicking heels as she marched over to the table, scooping up the plates.

The clattering of plates accompanied the clicking heels and the loading of the dishwasher provided its separate beat.

As Aoife walked to the sink with the cloth, she knew 'fine' didn't mean fine when Mummy said it like that and then she became confused because they didn't even have a dog.

12th December 20:03 Aoife

Mummy pulled Aoife's fairy duvet up over Aoife's shoulders, kissed her goodnight and said, "It's too late for a bedtime story tonight, pumpkin."

"Okay," Aoife replied and, smiling, she wrapped her small arms around her mummy's neck, inhaling her scent which to Aoife smelt like Christmas, Easter and birthdays and all of her favourite memories all at once.

Sometimes, Aoife could hear Mummy cry at night and wondered what it was she had done, promising herself that when she woke in the morning, she would be especially good and maybe Mummy's eyes would sparkle again; maybe Mummy would be happy in her heart again. Mummy did try to smile sometimes, but only managed to raise one corner of her lip and her eyes didn't smile at all.

12th December 21:23 Aoife

It was nearly Christmas but not in 34 Burgundy Road. The house was bare of decoration and on the 12th of December, the tree still wasn't up.

Aoife was sat on her bed. She had put on her favourite reindeer pyjamas, inside out, so the labels and seams didn't scratch. She propped her chin up with her knees so that the extra weight from the sadness in her head wouldn't make it fall off. If it did, then she wouldn't be able to look up through her window and say goodnight to the moon and the stars. She wouldn't be able to look out for Father Christmas and his reindeer and make a wish. She gasped, raising her small hand to her mouth.

Her long, auburn hair hung shrouding her face, creating a space in which she could hide away while she further contemplated the downside of losing her head.

Through her closed door, she could hear muffled raised voices. Mum and Dad were being cross again.

She should be asleep; it was way past her bedtime and Daddy had just got home. Aoife parted her auburn hair like a pair of curtains and looked up to her windowsill. The clock said 9:23. She had been in bed since 8:00.

When Aoife had asked Mummy earlier where Daddy was, Mummy had sat her down and hugged her so close that Aoife could hear the ba boom, ba boom of her heartbeat as Mummy explained, "Daddy has had a promotion and at this time of year, it's very busy at work." Aoife nodded even though she didn't understand what a 'permotion' was, so Mummy continued: "He is working very hard on a big account, so sometimes Daddy has to be at work late and sometimes he has to travel on a plane."

Aoife concentrated very hard, but she didn't know what a 'permotion' was or how bigger count it had to be. Opening her dictionary, she searched, but 'permotion' was not in the book. She knew what count was, so didn't need to check. She then wondered if he had to do a test like she had to do sometimes in Mrs Lesley's numeracy class.

She was sure Daddy knew how to count as they had played hide and seek lots of times, and he counted all the way to 50 once when she had told him she was going to hide behind the sofa. He had also helped her with her times-table once and he was good at that too. She sighed and wished she was a bit cleverer so that she could help him. She just needed to be seven years old. Because if she was seven, she was sure she would understand. But her birthday was ages away, in June.

Aoife decided not to ask Mummy about it again as she still remembered how her mummy's eyes were shiny like glass last time, and she had swallowed down the sadness, like Aoife had done sometimes when Tess had called her names.

Aoife tried hard not to listen to the muffled voices and as she started to say her 2 times table, the door opened. "Daddy?" she asked, flicking her auburn hair back. "Aubrey," she whispered. "What are you doing here again?" Aubrey remained silent as he walked towards her clutching Spark, his tatty green dragon which he had had since birth. As the door shut behind him, she heard her mum shout.

"You don't understand! I just can't find the Christmas Spirit!"

Aubrey climbed in to Aoife's bed and she tucked him and Spark under her duvet. Before slipping in to slumber, she smiled, she had made a plan.

13th December 06:45 Aoife

The morning started like every other morning. Aoife woke to the whispering of her name by Mummy and the biggest smile from Aubrey who was perched on Mummy's hip clutching Spark tightly in his left hand. As was the same most mornings, Aoife also woke wondering how Aubrey had managed to get out of her bed without her knowing.

However, unlike any other morning, Aoife jumped out of bed in a rush to start the day, Mummy didn't have to ask her to shower or brush her teeth, she didn't even have to force her in to her red, scratchy uniform with the labels unpicked because Aoife had a very important mission today. But first, she needed to get to school.

13th December 07:45 Jen

As Jen stood at the sink watching Aoife, she was grateful that this morning's routine was running so well. She had a deadline to submit her book draft. It was already one week overdue and her publisher was not best pleased.

Wrapping both hands around her large mug of coffee, she made her way to the living room.

Looking out over the garden, she observed the morning dew as it sat over the green like a blanket, white and yet transparent; and the moon danced, casting rays like a spotlight upon it. She shivered involuntarily, sipping on her coffee to warm her imaginary chill and her mind drifted towards the night before.

Their 10th wedding anniversary was spent separated by rooms, but in reality, the void was bigger than that. Their roads were veering off in different directions and she wasn't sure which of them chose it and when she had noticed.

She smiled and her eyes followed as she remembered that first day they met with much fondness.

She was sitting in her favourite cafe facing out to nature, giving her the illusion of being alone. It was a beautiful autumnal day and the leaves were spread like a blanket across the green backdrop of the grass. She had sipped her coffee, savouring that first drop where the cinnamon hit the back of her throat just like so many times before and afterwards. She watched the squirrels race up and down the trees and birds hopping along the ground until nature transported her to a place where all noise faded, and her imagination spilled on to the pages with each drop of ink. In that place, in that space, her pen created a whole new world of promise and possibility for her characters.

It was while in that moment, while her pen raced across the page as if it had life of its own, that she was jolted from her trance. She looked up and stared at him. His lips were moving, but the volume in the present and real world was still on mute.

"Is this seat taken?" the man asked.

Her brow furrowed, she looked around. The cafe was particularly busy that day so she reluctantly said, "No!" then proceeded to look down.

Her concentration was gone but she didn't want to engage with this man who had disturbed her flow. Although it hadn't escaped her how handsome he was. She had quickly chased the thought away in an attempt to get back to her story.

But then, Jen found herself very much in the present as she watched, as if in slow motion, the brown liquid splash across her pages, and as she looked across the table, the man was red-faced and apologetic, his mouth opening and shutting like a gold fish as he scrambled for the paper serviettes sat in the silver holder. His hands were suddenly across the page, mopping up the residue of his mocha choco latte in a futile attempt to remove all evidence of the disaster.

All she could do was stare, and eventually, the quiet fish-like motions of his mouth changed to the audible, "I'm so sorry, so sorry, I'm really sorry." The less she said, the more he repeated himself. She wasn't sure whether it was from hysteria of watching months of work disappearing under a brown damp mess or from the sheer devastation on his face, but she suddenly burst out laughing. She laughed so hard that she immediately began crying, so the man then proceeded to mop the tears from her eyes and that just made her cry even more.

Eventually, the laughing tears turned to sad tears and at that moment, she felt that she had just released months, if not years, of tension.

When she eventually stopped, he was still sitting opposite her, just staring. "I'm so sorry," he offered again and she put her hand up, unable to listen to one more sorry.

"I know," she said.

"Was it important?" he asked, immediately regretting it.

She threw him a glance that told him, "Yes."

"I'm so…"

"Sorry?" she finished, "I know, it's fine." Instinct told him, however, that wasn't so.

She composed herself and looked at him as if seeing him for the first time. His eyes looked sad and she could see the apology in them. His face was handsome but not pretty, and his smile was warming. "I'm Perry," he offered. She was still admiring the auburn hair so she didn't respond. He repeated the words, this time a smile upon his face and it was her turn to go red.

"Jen, Jennifer, I mean Jennifer but everyone calls me Jen," she said.

"Nice to meet you, Jennifer," he replied. They both laughed at their imperfect acquaintance.

Perry bought two more coffees as Jen placed her journal on the radiator to dry. Neither of them seemed to notice the passing of time, the comings and goings of customers and staff, and when the cafe closed, they both felt cheated out of conversation. The conversation had flowed easily and effortlessly. Jen didn't want to let him go, a feeling she had only ever explored in the words on the pages of the books that she wrote and which she had lived vicariously through.

They both walked towards Canada Water tube station side by side in silence until a glance and a "Goodbye". Perry's hotel was five minutes from the tube and she turned away from him and headed for the station's stairs.

The tap on her shoulder made her jump. She hadn't heard him coming, her head so full of internal dialogue. "Can I see you again?" Perry asked.

"Yes," was about all Jen could say. She hoped her heart wasn't jumping too far out of her chest, giving her away. Opening her bag, Jen held up her damaged journal and a pen. Perry wrote his number on a brown-stained page and, within moments, had disappeared in to the evening's shadows.

Jen barely remembered the journey to Greenwich. She barely remembered the short walk towards her flat. As she unlocked the door to her small abode, her valued space some-how felt a little empty that evening.

Jen texted Perry barely 30 minutes later and life for them began. That was 12 years ago and now.

"It's time to go, Mummy." Jen looked down; Aoife was pulling on her cardigan.

When Jen looked up at the clock, it was 8 a.m. She gulped her coffee down, wiped Aubrey's mouth with a flannel, lifted him from his seat and, at Aubrey's protests, went back for Spark. She grabbed the car keys from the tray in the hall and headed out of the door with her bag, scarf and coat.

Taking one look at the traffic, with Aubrey holding on to Aoife's hand, she raced back in, grabbed Aubrey's buggy and, strapping Aubrey in, they headed down the road, double speed, Aoife leading the way.

They arrived at Aoife's school two minutes before the line-up and Aoife blew her mummy a kiss as she raced to the front.

Jen continued to the nursery where she dropped Aubrey off. "Shall I take Spark home? He looks very tired," Jen offered Aubrey. Aubrey replied with a grimace and a shake of his head. Jen looked at Miss Johnson, his nursery teacher and mouthed, "Sorry," leaving Aubrey and Spark to enjoy their day.

Miss Johnson raised her over-elaborate eyebrow. Jen couldn't worry about her today, she had to get back to her book and her deadline.

Jen ran home pushing the empty buggy, unlocked the door and headed straight for her study which was more like a library.

She picked up her journal and brushed her hand over the embossed elephant cover. She had always enjoyed choosing a journal; telling her stories with pen and paper, it gave her the feeling of intimacy with her characters.

Setting her alarm clock for 2:30 pm, she sat at her desk to finish her novel.

13th December 08:43 Aoife

At school, Aoife watched the clock, the big hand was moving very slowly.

Mrs Lesley sat at her desk, her head slumped, resting on her hand as she drew or wrote, Aoife couldn't quite tell from her seat at the back of the classroom. Tess was throwing scrunched paper at Rory and Mrs Lesley wasn't saying anything.

Aoife glared at them, hoping the power of her thoughts would laser into the back of their heads and stop their naughtiness. She wondered whether she should tell Mrs Lesley what was happening, as she didn't seem to be noticing.

A sheet of paper lay on each desk upside down. The test would begin in two minutes. Aoife's hands were sweating and she could hear her heart beating. *What if Tess and Rory don't stop? Then I can't do my best,* she thought. Just then, Mrs Lesley stood up, a smile on her face but her eyes distant and dull, she said, "Turn your sheets over, children, and you can begin."

"Yes!" Aoife whispered, arm bent up and pulling down as if pulling on a lever, and she lifted her pencil and began to fill it in.

Mummy and Aubrey were waiting for her when she came out of school. Aubrey greeted her with his usual smile and she gave him and Spark a hug before wrapping her arms around her mummy's waist and pressing her head up against her stomach.

At home, Aoife changed in to her jogging bottoms wearing them inside out, her pockets on show and her cotton unicorn top smooth upon her skin. She wrapped her scarf around her neck, put on her boots and she headed for the back door to begin her search.

With her hand on the door handle, she stopped in her tracks. "Aoife, where are you going?" Mummy was standing right behind her.

"I'm going to play in my hut," Aoife replied.

"Okay, but it's cold, don't stay out too long."

At that moment, Aubrey, who had been sat on the sofa watching Teletubbies, appeared from behind Jen and headed straight towards Aoife, "Can I come?"

Aoife looked at her mummy, hoping she could read her plea. She didn't and said, "Okay, but you'll have to get your coat and hat, Aubrey."

Aoife huffed a little and when Aubrey reappeared, she held on to his hand and attempted to hurry him and Spark to the bottom of the garden. As they walked, ice crunched underfoot and Aubrey pulled himself loose to jump; smashing through it. When he laughed, Aoife lost her urgency and joined in for a minute.

13th December 16:00 Jen

Jen looked out of the window of her study. She smiled when she saw Aoife and Aubrey jumping outside. She watched Aoife's waist-length hair bounce up and down in the cold winter haze and watched Aubrey throw Spark in the air, failing to catch him every time. She smiled, feeling a warm rush of pure love fill her up. Then looking at the time, Jen sat back down and immersed herself in her work. Her novel was nearly finished. *Twenty more minutes of editing,* she thought.

13th December 16:05 Aoife

Aoife opened the door to the hut and Aubrey walked straight over to the bench. He sat Spark at the table and placed a wooden plate and a plastic cup in front of him before rummaging through the treasures in the bench.

Aoife walked over to the wooden kitchen, which Father Christmas had bought her last year, and took out her picnic basket from inside the oven. At the bottom of the basket, she found Stick. Placing Stick on the table, she explained, "Stick, we're going on an adventure. We need to find the Christmas Spirit and I don't know what she looks like."

At this point, Aubrey stopped rummaging and asked, "What's Crismas spit?"

"Christmas Spirit," Aoife pronounced slowly and Aubrey stared at her but didn't repeat it.

"I don't know," Aoife replied, "but Mummy said she can't find it, so I have to."

"Aubrey come!" Aubrey exclaimed.

"No, Aubrey, it's too cold, you need to stay here." Turning to face him, she said in her softest big sister voice, "Don't tell anybody what I'm doing, it's a surprise."

"What's a sprise?" Aubrey asked, returning her gaze.

She looked up, eyes focused, as she searched, seemingly plucking words from the air. "It's ummm, it's like when somebody gives you a present," Aoife said. "You can see the pretty paper, but you don't know what's inside it cause it's a surprise."

"Okay," Aubrey replied and continued to rummage in his bench, bringing out a train, a teddy and a Barbie doll with her legs pulled off. Aubrey then walked over to the kitchen, picked up the teapot and wooden fruit, made a feast for Spark,

Teddy and Barbie while he drove the train around the table with 'choo choo' sound effects.

Aoife found her unicorn rucksack and placed Stick inside. She then played with Aubrey until the door swung outward and Mummy bent over, poking her head inside. "It's getting very cold, children. Come on in, dinner's ready."

Aoife helped Aubrey put his toys away. She placed her basket back in the wooden oven and put her rucksack on her back before heading out of the door behind Aubrey.

Aubrey stood in front of his mummy holding up his hands, "Carry!"

"Carry!" Jen swooped Aubrey up and he pressed himself up against her, nuzzling into her neck to warm himself.

As Aoife strolled behind, she felt the wind sting her face and noticed how the moon lit a path to the backdoor. She smiled up at twinkling stars and the waxing crescent moon before heading in to the warmth. She knew all about the moon from the book on her bedside table and Mummy had told her all about the constellations.

Aoife remembered how she and Mummy used to always look at the stars at bedtime, and Aoife would make her explain over and over about the biggest and brightest one.

"That one," Mummy would say, pointing up through the window, "that big star is the North Star and it sits above the North Pole, but what makes it special is that it doesn't appear to move," she'd say. "It's also the tip of the handle of the Little Dipper constellation. The Little Dipper looks like a ladle but that's not all."

Mummy would say, "The Little Dipper also forms part of the tail of the Little Bear," and then she would look at Aoife, her eyes wide, smiling, and Aoife would smile back, thinking her mummy was the cleverest, most specialist Mummy in the world.

Mummy had told her that story so many times, Aoife could hear her voice every day when she said goodnight to the moon and the stars.

13th December 19:00 Aoife

Daddy arrived home at 7 pm and there were no cross words.

"How was your day, pumpkin?" he asked, looking at Aoife.

"Good," Aoife replied. "I got a sticker today."

"Wow, what for?" Mummy asked."

"The best sums," she said, smiling, looking directly at her daddy. "I can help you Daddy if you want. I can even do my four times table."

Looking a little bemused, Perry replied, "Thank you, pumpkin, I'll bear that in mind."

While snuggled on the sofa together, watching Aubrey's favourite programme 'In the Night Garden', Aoife stood up and announced, "I'm going to bed now."

Jen and Perry looked at one another surprised, "Okay, pumpkin, do you want a story?" Daddy asked, getting up off the sofa.

"No, thank you, I'm a bit tired."

"Okay," Mummy replied, "come and give me a kiss." Aoife rushed over and wrapped her arms around her mummy's neck and whispered, "Goodnight, Mummy." She did the same to her daddy.

13th December 19:10 Jen

Jen sat quietly, realising she hadn't even asked her children about their day. In fact, when had she last really engaged and asked them about anything? The book had taken most of her focus and then there were the constant spats with Perry which usually started before he got home as he texted or spouted one reason or ten why he would be late again. In Jen's mind, it mostly translated to level of importance and priority and, somehow, she was slipping right down a long list of both.

But right now, Jen felt a big pang of guilt. She promised herself she'd work on a positive mindset in the morning now that her novel was complete and the pressure alleviated.

13th December 19:15 Aoife

After brushing her teeth, Aoife reached under her bed and picked up her rucksack, removing Stick. She then walked to her drawers, pulled out her favourite snowman jumper and a pair of fluffy socks that looked like Christmas stockings and pushed them in to her bag.

She wanted Father Christmas to see the jumper and socks he had given her last year.

She then emptied her piggy bank and placed her coins in the front pocket of her rucksack. She then pushed her bottle of water into the side pocket. Then Aoife placed Stick on top of her clothes before zipping it up.

Aoife then climbed onto her bed and looked outside. "Hello, Mr Moon, I need your help. I am going to find the Christmas Spirit. I'm a little bit scared of the dark so please, can you shine your light?" Looking up, she then found the brightest star, the North Star and said, "North Star, I'm going to follow you. I need to find Father Christmas in the North Pole so that he can tell me where the Christmas Spirit lives because he knows all about Christmas." She was sure that the moon smiled and the star winked, so Aoife trusted that they would do as she asked.

Setting her alarm, like Mummy had shown her, Aoife snuggled under her duvet in her clothes and slept until 2 a.m., when she was pulled from her dream by the music of her favourite superhero's theme tune.

Aoife tiptoed out of her room and walked towards the front door where she carefully removed her coat, picked up her boots and hat, and then tiptoed to the backdoor. She pulled on her boots, hat and coat, and hung the rucksack on her back before walking down the garden under the moonlight towards the North Star.

At the bottom of the garden, she removed her rucksack and pushed it through the broken fence onto the field behind, before squeezing through the gap herself. She ripped her coat on a nail and was worried that Mummy would be even sadder, but she carried on walking, knowing Father Christmas would be able to help them all. Once in the field, she removed Stick from her rucksack and they continued across the field towards the North Star.

She was sure Stick would help her find Father Christmas, as well as water if she didn't have enough in her unicorn bottle.

She remembered picking up Stick on a walk through the woods and her daddy telling her how clever sticks can be and that in the olden days, people used them to find water underground. She can't remember what the name was but she thought Stick must be very special if he could do that, so she brought him home and let him live in her basket, in her wooden oven which Father Christmas had made for her.

14th December 05:00 Perry

Perry woke with the alarm at 5 a.m. Looking over at his wife, her hair draped down her back, he watched the rise and fall of her body as she slept soundly. He loved her and missed them.

He rose, making his way to the shower, promising himself that he would take some time out once he had finished the project for the Sealsy account. His entire team were throwing 100% at it all of the time and he knew it wasn't sustainable, but a final extra push towards Christmas and the work will be done. *Who was he kidding?* he thought.

As he did most mornings, afternoons and evenings, seven days a week, he stepped through his schedule mentally.

Today is important on my list of already important, pressing tasks! he thought with a little sarcasm mixing the words.

He sighed just thinking about it. Glancing at his watch, he realised, "They'll just about be landing now," he said it out loud in a whisper. He was doing that often lately, having a conversation with himself and catching himself doing it, wondering when it started.

The CEO and CFO of Kirstin & Klein were paying their annual visit to London, where the ritual of PowerPoint forecasts and a tango around the prosperity and longevity of keeping their business in London would ensue before the frivolity of a Christmas party, where everyone inevitably drank too much, and for a small percentage of time, felt honoured to be celebrating in the same space as their founders who dished out platitudes and promises of wonderful times ahead, looking their employees square in the eyes as they shook their hands.

Behind closed doors, Brexit was waved around like a samurai sword cutting the discussion to the quick on the topic of budget, investment and particularly salaries and bonuses.

Perry had lost two very good people to competitors this past year with the inflexible stance of the CEO and CFO who focused on the bottom line and not who got them there.

Perry could almost hear Mike Klein tutting and spouting, "Well, you know, Perry, these are worrying times for the financial market instability and a prime minister that's quite frankly making the UK the laughing stock," as he picked up another glass of champagne to wash his Lobster Thermidor down, never quite finishing a point he was going to make.

Perry was well aware of the news and the views of those looking in, but the fact was that Kirstin & Klein were more profitable now than they had ever been, so fearmongering and fairytale predictions were just another stick to beat them with.

Isn't it honestly the case that nobody knows what the fallout from Brexit will be? he thought. *How can they make such sweeping statements when the politicians haven't even squared that circle?*

If there was evidence to be dished, then the truth is the figures in the here and now, the figures about the growth of Kirstin & Klein on this island, speak for themselves.

For two years, the threat of relocation has hung over the workforce; a fluctuation in the stock market inevitably resulted in panic waves crossing digitally from the headquarters in Washington to his inbox as Roberta Kirstin sends another Access programme link for suggested cost cuttings which she had been working on all night, reminding him to keep the shareholders happy and the profits up.

This year's Christmas party will be less extravagant again. They'd opted for contract caterers and a buffet in the large board meeting room. Champagne was substituted for sparkling wine and the bonuses for the workforce had been halved. He would have the pleasure of announcing that this evening.

Perry was finding it increasingly, morally difficult to justify demanding all hands-on deck for a 15 hour/day when their reward was life imbalance and time off with stress. Husbands missing wives, parents missing out on children's plays, as he will this year.

He could feel his pulse racing again and so he took a deep breath.

He thought about his beautiful, bright Aoife; she had only wanted to be the star in the play and he remembered receiving a text from Jen with a picture of Aoife bursting with joy having just been given the good news by Mrs Lesley that she'd got the part.

He stood facing the mirror, staring, his razor firm in his hand and he examined his face. "There will be more nativities," he told himself.

Dark shadows sat permanently under his eyes as if to accentuate the exhaustion he was feeling physically and emotionally, while the frown lines had multiplied and were chiselled deep set above his brow.

A side-effect to persistent pushing and striving, he thought. Sometimes, however, he wasn't even sure what he was striving for.

He hadn't planned for success. Planning was Jen's department.

He seemed to roll into positions because he was good at what he did. He certainly had a Midas touch and soft skills, but promotions meant he invariably worked long hours and even the weekends were consumed by trying to fit in downtime, ready for the sprint on Monday again.

Perry slipped in to the suit and shirt he had hung out the night before and grabbed his favourite silk tie, yellow-striped with a hidden message sewn inside. 'I believe in you,' it said and he recalled how Jen had handed it to him for his 37th birthday and had made him look for it. It seemed so childish then, frustrating even, but now it's all he remembers and the one thing he brings with him when he needs strength. He took one last look in the mirror under the dim light, stroked his tie flat and with a backward glance at his sleeping wife, he headed towards the kitchen.

A quick look at the clock sent alarm bells ringing as he was late, so he headed straight for the door, slipped in to his shoes and grabbed his long black, woollen coat and scarf.

He shivered slightly stood in the hall and as he opened the door, he was greeted by a glistening sheet of ice which had collected on the drive. He tiptoed across and once on the gritted path, made haste towards the bus stop on Cranberry Road.

14th December 06:15 Jen

Jen woke with the sound of music blasting from the radio. She was a creature of habit and set her alarm to James Brown's 'Get On Up' every morning.

This morning, the house was quiet, not a stir coming from Aubrey, so she danced to the shower in her bra and knickers, singing along to James Brown's rasping tones.

Ten minutes later, she was dressed and heading for Aubrey. She would give Aoife ten more minutes to sleep.

Aubrey greeted Jen with a huge smile and the usual mess around his bed. He had a routine of rummaging through his toy box and removing most items by simply throwing them in backward motion across the room. He then sat in among the chaos and began playing with all of them, Spark always close beside him. She left him to play for a few moments longer while she ran a bath.

In a well-rehearsed manner, Jen whipped him up off the floor, helped him remove his pyjamas and put him in the bath with Ducky and a ball. Aubrey then proceeded to try to hit Ducky with the ball, giggling as the water splashed on his face and up his nose. A short while later, she had wrapped him in his grey, hooded towel and they were back in the bedroom, dressing him for nursery.

In the kitchen, Jen strapped Aubrey in to his booster seat, placed the cut slices of fruit in front of him and lay a separate bowl on the table for Aoife. She then placed the bread in the toaster, switched the coffee machine on, noting that Perry must have been late again as that was his only morning job, and she headed towards Aoife's room.

When she reached Aoife's bedroom, the first thing she noticed was the door was ajar. *I must have forgotten to close it,* she thought, and mentally walked through the events of the night before's routines while at the same time, pushing it open. Jen wasn't sure how long it took her mind to register but from that moment, events went in slow motion.

Aoife's bed was slept in but Aoife wasn't in bed. She called Aoife's name while heading quick-paced towards the en-suite. Had Aoife been silly and run her own shower? *She was growing up fast,* Jen thought to herself, and the thought immediately passed when she stood staring at an empty bathroom. Jen could hear her heartbeat loud in her ears, fog was descending where logic once prevailed. Coming out of the room, she smiled at Aubrey, all the time fighting the urge to panic.

Pull yourself together, she'll be in the office or in our room, she won't have gone far. As the muscles in her legs began to turn to jelly, Jen ran to her bedroom calling Aoife's name as softly as she could so that she didn't upset her sensitive child.

She opened cupboards, slammed them closed. "Coming, ready or not," she announced which came out as a squeak while she waited for Aoife to jump out from behind the sofa, behind the curtains.

Nothing! She checked the office, under the beds and then all of the rooms again, imagining whether she could have slipped past trying to outwit Jen. Aubrey was watching her. Jen's face and actions no longer the picture of calm and control.

"Fifi coming, Mummy?" Aubrey asked.

"In a minute, in a minute," is all Jen could manage as she headed for the hall. "Think, think, think…" Jen couldn't, the fog had settled on rationale and she couldn't fight it. Breathe, breathe, breathe…Aoife…coat, Aoife's coat was missing. Jen looked down. Aoife's boots were missing, Aoife's scarf was missing. With some relief, Jen put two and two together. She's in the hut.

Jen put on her boots running through the house, *which was against the house rules*, she thought, and then chased it away. *This called for emergency measures*, she thought and she pulled the backdoor open and raced to the bottom of the garden, nearly slipping on the ice. Bending over, she pulled open the door to the hut and there she was met by darkness and an emptiness which described well what she was feeling inside now.

Her screams pierced the morning mist, drowning out her thinking space.

All rationale had left her. She looked around the garden. It felt like she was at the centre of a merry-go-round, the garden spinning around her faster and faster as her anxiety grew—haunting and desperate.

The scream pierced through the morning sky, drowning out the silence, filling Jen's head with its echo as it bounced around, volume too high, volume too loud, and just one word over and over and over, "AOIFE!"

From within another voice came, *Shut up, shut up…I can't think.*

All at once, Jen fell silent. The muscles in her legs had finally refused to hold her up and she fell down on the frozen ground unable to think.

Think, think…

Dave, Jen's elderly neighbour, was shouting over the fence, "Jen, what's the matter? Jen? Jen!"

When he received no response, he ran up his garden, letting himself in through Jen's side gate. When he arrived, Jen was on her way up to the house. "Jen, what's wrong?"

"Aoife, Aoife," she couldn't seem to say anymore.

Aubrey was still strapped in his booster seat, his fruit and bowl strewn separately across the kitchen floor. She smiled at him belying her true emotions and Aubrey responded with tears.

Jen stared at him unable to comfort him, willing herself to pull herself together. "Phone, where's my phone?"

Rationale was trying to resume its rightful place.

Dave was behind her. "Where's Perry?"

Jen stared at him, no words coming out of her mouth. "Jen, where's Perry?" Dave repeated.

Nothing! Jen proceeded to look for her phone. It was in the kitchen next to the coffee machine. She picked it up and rang Perry. It went straight to voice. She dialled 999.

"Hello, what's your emergency?"

The police were on Jen's doorstep in 23 minutes. By this time, Perry had still not been reached.

14th December 08:19 Perry

Perry took his mobile phone out of his pocket as he walked through the rotating doors of his office, still frustrated by the consistent delays of the trains and tubes.

He opened the case and glancing down, he saw 22 missed calls and four voice mails on the screen. It wasn't unusual for him to have a number of missed calls, but 22 at this time of the morning was a little excessive.

Just as he went to click on voice mail, he noticed Gary, his personal assistant, rushing towards him. Perry suppressed a smile; he'd never seen Gary move so fast. Gary was a short, rotund man who took his time over everything but yet here he was hurrying, and it was a little disconcerting for Perry.

"Everything okay, Gary?"

"Umm, Jen has been trying to contact you, it's urgent," Perry went to speak but Gary continued quickly, almost spewing the words out, "and…there's a police officer here to see you, Perry," he replied.

"Me?"

"Hello, Mr Mercier, my name's Judy Vincent," the officer said, getting to her feet.

"I'm sorry," Perry interrupted, raising his hand to stop her, "I'll be with you in a minute, I have to phone my wife and I'm afraid I have to get to a meeting. What's this about please?" Perry asked.

A million thoughts ran through Perry's mind: *What had he forgotten to do that was so urgent that Jen needed to get hold of him? Was Jen okay? The kids?*

Judy gestured with her hand, "Mr Mercier…Perry, please take a seat, this won't take a minute."

Perry felt like he had been sat in front of the headteacher and he waited, his gaze on her and then looking down at his watch.

None of what he had thought prepared him for what was coming out of the PC's mouth. She was talking about Aoife and Jen, missing and search, and it all was a little discombobulated; *jumbled words,* he thought. He deliberated over that word, slowly dissecting it syllable by syllable. Dis com bob u late, then snapped back in to consciousness—terrifying real life.

Words which had hung in the air dropped and joined up in his mind in full unfathomable sentences. *What did the officer mean Aoife is missing? They had the wrong man, the wrong Aoife, the wrong Jen, the wrong house, the wrong universe, the…Aoife is missing!*

"Perry, did you see Aoife this morning?" Judy asked. Perry shook his head.

Gary sat beside Perry, propping him up. Perry couldn't hear the officer anymore. He watched her lips move…he noticed her blinking and that she was picking at her nails, but the world around him had become a silent movie. Gary's mouth was moving, "Perry, Perry." The sound seeped in and the volume went up and his mind began whirling.

He had an important meeting this morning and looking at Gary, he was in a dilemma and he hated that he was giving the thought traction. He went to speak, "Perry, go home. I'll sort this."

Gary swallowed the lump in his throat as he watched Perry walk away. He had never seen his boss like that.

Perry was always in control. The man in front of him here was lost, childlike and very vulnerable.

On his way to the car with Judy, Perry picked up the phone and called Jen.

"Do you have her with you? Tell me she's with you, Perry, tell me…" Jen pleaded.

Perry had never heard such desperation from his wife. "No, Jen," he responded. "Is she…"

"I've looked everywhere, she isn't playing hide and seek," Jen interrupted and there it was again, silence, long and stretched, and yet so much was understood in that space. Jen spoke first, "Hurry home, I have to go. The police…"

"I will…" Perry said hanging up.

14th December 02:25 Aoife

Aoife was cold so she wrapped her scarf tighter around herself. She felt as though she had been walking for a long time. She had walked this way with Mummy before and knew where she would come out, and when she reached the back of her school, she could see the clock in the playground and it said 2:25.

She took a little break and sat on the red, plastic seat in the bus shelter, wondering whether she would be home for dinner as she was a little bit hungry. She thought her trip to the North Pole could take her ages, at least a day.

Sat at the bus stop, she heard the jingle of a bell. *Huh, a reindeer,* she thought, excitement filling her imagination. As she stood up, she noticed a small dog sniffing around the bin outside of the bus shelter. "Hello," she said, keeping her distance, remembering her mummy and daddy had always told her to be careful of stroking dogs as they might not always be friendly.

The dog looked up at her wagging its tail before taking another sniff around the bin and the shelter. Bored with that, the dog, who Aoife noticed was wearing a blue collar with a silver bell, walked over to Aoife. Not only was its tail wagging, but the whole of his bottom joined in the excitement.

"Hello," Aoife said again. "What's your name?" she looked for a name tag like Luna, her friend Elsie's dog, but she couldn't find one. "You should go home," Aoife said. "It's a bit cold."

Getting up, Aoife said, "Bye," and headed towards the North Star. The dog, however, didn't go home, it followed and Aoife had mixed feelings of worry and gratitude at having a friend. Turning around, she explained to the dog, "I'm going to call you Gingerbread," and then proceeded to tell Gingerbread where she was heading.

Gingerbread looked at Aoife attentively, moving his head from side to side, ears pricked up as if listening to every word. When Aoife had finished explaining, they continued on their walk.

At the end of Cranberry Road was St Francis Church. She loved the church; she loved the patterns on the windows, the images stained within them and the way the light changed colour when it shone through. The high ceiling made the room so big and the voices saying a prayer or singing echoed, bouncing off the walls, making it feel like the congregation was much bigger than it was. She had been to Sunday school once with Elsie and they made cards, did painting, drank orange juice and she ate a rich tea biscuit. She wished she could go again another day.

Looking around the square, Aoife was a little disappointed that the Christmas lights weren't on. When Mummy had taken her to see the carol singers last week, she had stared at them hard and their rays had stretched longer and longer, joining together as if a long tip of a witch's finger were touching another.

Other times, her eyes less tense, she imagined them to be stars twinkling, almost reachable as she stretched her arms up then jumped to grasp them. When she couldn't reach, she closed her eyes and concentrated very hard, trying to summon a unicorn to whisk her up so that she could fly over the top of the town, higher than the tip of the church, and watch from above, taking a picture with her mind so that she may let the image come to life on her sketchpad.

But the unicorn didn't come and so she drew that picture from her imagination, imagining also that Father Christmas and his reindeer will see the square, the same way when he flies over on Christmas Eve.

Other than the chatter in her mind which her memories had evoked in that place where she stood, the only sound was the whooshing of the wind whispering in her ears and snapping at her face with its frozen embrace. The bell around Gingerbread's neck accompanied its menace, and the shuffling sound of her footsteps differed between the hard pavement and the ice which rested as a glistening sheet upon it.

Aoife walked up the path towards the entrance of the church and pushed on the door with both hands pressed against its oak. It was locked.

Aoife hung her head and her mouth displayed disappointment, and she continued on her way towards the North Star down Mortimer Avenue.

She looked up at the tall trees bare of leaves that looked as though they had been sketched with black pen onto the landscape. A few lanterns cast shadows across the road and up the big houses and in the distance, Aoife heard a car and a dog barking.

She looked down at Gingerbread who had continued to follow, sniffing trees and grass as he went. In her hand, she still held Stick tightly. At the bottom of Mortimer Avenue Aoife had to decide to take a left or right turn. The North Star was straight ahead. She had never walked this far before it was making her legs ache.

"Gingerbread, which way?" she delegated. Gingerbread simply looked up at Aoife, his head cocked to the side and his ears pricked but no barks of wisdom passed his lips. So, Aoife held Stick like Daddy had taught her and waited for Stick to decide what way next.

Stick wobbled a little but then pointed left. So, Aoife continued to walk left. She was no longer sure what the name of the road was and if she was honest, Aoife was feeling a bit scared. But she could still see her mummy's sad face and she told herself to be brave. Aoife had been walking a while when she saw a road that went straight down towards the North Star again. She looked left and right, and crossed over the road she had been walking down.

Stood on the opposite side of the road, she called, "Gingerbread, Ginnngerrrbreead, come on." Gingerbread was distracted sniffing the stump of a tree, lost in the moment.

On the third call, Gingerbread pricked up his ears and raced straight across the road. Aoife then proceeded to lecture him on how that was wrong and how he needed to check and not just run. Gingerbread simply looked at Aoife wagging his entire rear. Bending over, Aoife stroked Gingerbread's head and they continued on their quest.

14th December 03:22
Jeanne Taylor

Jeanne Taylor swore she could hear a young girl's voice shouting. Her gaze fell on the clock, 3:22 a.m., before lifting her head from her pillow to listen again.

Silence.

Walking to her window, looking up and down Dalton Road, she caught a glimpse of a dog walking down Mill Hill Farm Road, but there was no sign of a little girl. She deduced that Jim and Jinny's grandchildren must be over again and so she fell back in to a deep sleep.

14th December 03:29 Aoife

Aoife was getting very tired and she was very cold. She couldn't feel her toes. At the end of the road across the field, Aoife saw a barn in the distance, lit up by the light of the moon.

She crossed the field, ice slippery, cracking underfoot and the damp from the cold puddles underneath seeped through her brown faux fur-lined boots.

The wind raced across the field as if in a rush to catch her; it wrapped its invisibility around her as it bit at her cheeks, snapped at her gloves, found its way into the gaps around her neck and hugged her wet feet in its chilling embrace, not letting up.

Aoife shook then looked down to outwit the wind but, in a mocking display, it changed direction and blew the dusting of snow from the ground up into her face as it raced past, rushing through the trees and shaking them; the little ones bent while the others shook like maracas but still, the wind blew stronger and faster, stinging her eyes until they wept.

So, she lifted her scarf with her frozen fingers and covered all but her eyes as she pressed forward to the barn.

Inside the barn, the game of tag ceased as the wind hit a wall of straw, unable to penetrate it. Aoife climbed up into the corner of the barn onto a bale, pulled her knees under her chin and wrapped her arms around her legs to keep her warm, but the wind pursued its game, finding its way through the broken roof and the gaps between the walls of wood.

Once Gingerbread had assessed the barn, sniffing his way up and down, he, too, jumped onto the straw bales and sat next to Aoife.

Aoife pressed her back up against a bale and Gingerbread leaned in. It was the first time Aoife had seen Gingerbread up close. He had two different eye colours, one blue and one grey and the longest eyelashes Aoife had ever seen. By now, Aoife was shivering, her teeth chattering.

She put Stick down, opened her bag and took out her socks and jumper. With shaking hands, she pulled her boots off and removed her wet socks, her feet were wrinkled and red, she couldn't feel them.

She pulled on her thick Christmas socks and then tried to clasp her zip with her fingers, but they were sore and unable to bend so she clasped her hands together and blew into them like Mummy and Daddy did when they've played in the snow.

After some time, she managed to pull the zip of her coat down, slip it off and pull the Christmas jumper over her head and over the unicorn top she was wearing. Aoife then pulled her coat back on, but couldn't close the zip as the extra layer was too thick underneath. She felt a little warmer and lay down on the bale.

Thirsty, she reached for her water bottle. It wasn't there. She'd lost it. As she closed her eyes, she thought, *Stick will help me later.* Tiredness pulled Aoife into its grasp almost instantly.

14th December 09:00 Jen

It was 9 a.m. and Jen's shock had now surpassed and had been replaced by lioness prowess. She tapped into her analytical mind as if she were following one of her characters through a plot, and she retraced her steps from the moment she had collected Aoife and Aubrey, recounting and recalling conversations, big and small, as she sat on Aoife's bed with her eyes closed. *Think, think, think…*

Dave, her elderly neighbour, had taken Aubrey to nursery to keep him away from the commotion at 34 Burgundy Road. Jen wasn't sure whether she had done the right thing but she simply told Aubrey that Aoife was staying at a friend's and "Silly Mummy forgot".

Aubrey had smiled, searching Jen's face as if seeing into her soul as he always did, and Jen prayed that he would believe her white lie through her beaming smile.

Aubrey went willingly with Dave and his wife Laura, and they even offered to pick him up if that would be helpful. Under normal circumstances, Jen would refuse all help. She was a firm believer of 'getting on by yourself' just like her parents and the generation before.

That good, old, stiff upper lip that was part of the McKinley DNA. But here and now, faced with a missing child—with her missing child—well, she would make a plea with the devil himself to bring her home safe.

The police officer, Harjot, was in his 40s, she guessed. He wore a turban and she estimated he was around six feet. She'd never been good at guessing and recalled the blinds she had bought that covered more than the window they were measured for.

She could see Perry now in stitches as he watched them being hung with a six-inch overlap each side. She wished he was here now.

Harjot stood in front of her with a milky tea in his hand in Perry's cup. Should she tell him that drinks aren't allowed in the bedroom or that she prefers her tea strong or that Perry doesn't like his cup being used?

Looking at him, his face overflowing with kindness and sympathy, she decided none of that mattered and she began sipping the warm, sweet liquid while chastising herself for even caring.

Her eyes took inventory as she scoured the length and breadth of Aoife's bedroom. There was something bothering her, something wasn't quite right, but the rewind of her mind hadn't identified exactly what was out of place. "Think, think Jen, think," she whispered under her breath.

Jen placed the tea on the set of drawers and looked under the bed then walked to the hall. Looking at the second police officer, she said, "Her bag, Aoife's unicorn bag, she brought it up from the hut, it's gone." Then she raced back into the bedroom, both police officers close behind.

Opening the drawers, Jen realised what had gone. "Aoife's Christmas socks, the ones that look like Christmas stockings and a jumper, ummm, think, Jen, think, her blue snowman jumper, they've gone."

14th December 09:15 Perry

In the police car, Perry's mind wandered as he attempted to replay the evening's events. He was struggling to breathe. Slipping his fingers between his neck and collar, he pulled on his shirt, he was choking.

Judy pressed the button to lower the passenger-side window before turning into the side road and safely bringing the car to a stop. Perry slumped sideways, his head resting near the open window trying to fill up on oxygen. He felt depleted. *How had she got out? Had somebody got in? Who had taken his baby girl? Why?* unanswered questions spun around and around. "I can't breathe," he said, wondering whether this was it. He was having that heart attack Jen kept suggesting he would with the level of work and stress.

"Perry, you're having a panic attack, look at me…breathe…" Judy demonstrated. Perry concentrated copying her actions…through the nose and out through the mouth, through the nose and out through the mouth until a rhythm was established, just like they had taught Aoife when she had reached a state of being overwhelmed.

Perry pressed his head up against the back of his seat and slowly steadied his breathing. When Judy saw his breathing stabilise, she asked, "Okay, to continue?" Perry nodded and Judy turned the key and drove onward.

"Let's run through it again. When did you last see Aoife?" Judy asked in an attempt to see whether any fresh light could be shed on this missing child.

"Ummm, it was around midnight," he said, "I usually go to bed around midnight, I always say goodnight…" and then as if to reinforce again, "I always say goodnight before I go to bed."

Perry fell silent for a moment as he recalled how he'd brushed Aoife's auburn hair from her face.

"Perry, anything else?" Judy asked.

"I kissed Aoife's cheek…"

Judy nodded. "Go on," she urged.

"No, that's it. I closed her curtains, whispered goodnight and left closing the door behind me," Perry responded.

He was scanning the recess of his mind for people who may have grudges against him. *Had he upset somebody? Presented wrong figures to them? Not signed off on expenses? Not given a high enough bonus?* He was giving himself a headache, hyperventilating in his own movie clips and reasoning and his plot was weak. He was a finance director of a reputable cooperation, not a fraudsters money man.

It took Judy a long time to negotiate the London traffic. Perry could recall as a child how cool it would have been to sit in a police car, sirens blaring; and here he sat, sirens screaming at passing drivers, making pedestrians jump, and he would give anything to be on the outside wondering what emergency somebody else was heading in to. He hated himself immediately for wishing this pain upon somebody else. Perry had to compose himself, he'd be home soon.

And here, he stood peeking into Aoife's room, watching Jen pull open drawers before getting on her hands and knees turning out beds, emptying out bins.

Finding a picture of Father Christmas, which Aoife had drawn, Jen paused for a moment as she rubbed her fingers across the drawing and Perry observed the police officers as they looked on in quiet contemplation, waiting for a morsel of a clue as to where she had gone.

Seeing Perry, Jen locked into his gaze, only offering, "The backdoor was unlocked this morning, the key was in it."

"But," Perry said, pausing as he thought, "I locked it and put the key in the tray."

At that moment, it occurred to him that the key tray once too high for the children was easily within his six-year-old daughter's reach. He could see that Jen had drawn the same conclusion; much was evident in their silence.

Everything went so fast after that. The doorbell rang and Harjot went and answered.

14th December 09:45
The Inspector

"Mr Mercier, this is Inspector Johnson."

"Tom please, no need for formalities," the inspector interjected.

Harjot continued, "The inspector…Tom has a number of police officers with him that will begin the search."

"Yes, of course," Perry responded, "I'll come now."

"It's best if you stay here in case she comes back. We'll let you know when we need you. An AMBER alert has been raised so we have officers up and down the country checking, and the alarms will be raised at the borders. Your wife gave us a picture earlier and that will be with every police station up and down the country now," Tom replied.

Perry just listened, taking it all in, his mind fixated on which picture that would be. Was it the one with the missing teeth? He so loved that picture.

"Excuse me," he said as he raced down the corridor. In his bathroom he was sick. "Pull yourself together, Perry," he chastised and washed his face with cold water. When he turned around, Jen was standing behind him.

They held on to one another tight; no words were exchanged, no words could fill the emptiness. No pen to rewrite the chapter, no plot to write the end. They stood in one another's grasp, powerless and speechless, and in those moments, they understood more than they had in years.

14th December 10:00
The Search

Jen's stories rarely took the path her readers hoped. There was no obvious and no happy endings for all of her characters but here in her own story, in the midst of the pain so unfathomable, she prayed for a happy ending, she willed a happy ending to bring Aoife home.

By 10 a.m., the story of their missing daughter had broken on the local radio.

By 10 a.m., their neighbours had been woken and their gardens searched. Judy sat Perry and Jen down and showed them the small piece of blue fabric the search party had found on their fence at the end of the garden.

Perry and Jen stared at each other, and Jen reached over and rubbed the fabric between her fingers.

Breaking the silence, she said, "It looks like it's from Aoife's coat." Judy nodded, stood back up and walked to the end of the garden where Tom stood and confirmed they had another lead. The search party continued into the field.

The search party continued past the primary school. The head mistress had been notified to keep the children in to avoid distress, and Mrs Lesley watched from the window, a tear rolling down her cheek as she wished Aoife home safe. She was still watching when the search party disappeared towards the town centre.

The small town-centre had been cordoned off by the time the search party arrived. As they approached the church entrance, one of the search party noticed a unicorn water bottle lying in front of a headstone. The bottle was bagged and given to an officer and ten minutes later, Judy was on her way back to the Mercier's residence.

At 34 Burgundy Road with the search party gone, you could hear a pin drop as Jen and Perry sat close, consumed by their own thoughts. Perry and Jen were advised that a family liaison officer was on the way.

Harjot was positioned outside the front door keeping the wolves out.

14th December 10:45
Jen and Perry

Jen was pacing and Perry, who sat paralysed by his feelings of uselessness, stood up and headed towards the front door. One hand unhooked his coat as the other pulled the door open. As he did, he came face to face with Judy. Behind her, he could see photographers and journalists camped on the pavement. "Any news, Mr Mercier? Perry, any leads?" Words tripping over themselves, hanging in the air as the gathering of men and women fought for their story. Perry dropped his coat back onto its peg and stepped back as Judy made her way through the opening.

In the kitchen, Judy and Perry were joined by Jen. Judy showed them the bottle and asked, "Do you recognise it?"

"Aoife has the same…" Jen headed for the cupboard. Opening the bottom left cupboard, she said, "It's not here." Taking a closer look at the bottle in the bag, she noticed the chewed lid and turned it upside down. She could see the last remnants of the permanent marker which had once spelt AM. Now the A was long gone and the M barely consisted of three dots. "It's Aoife's," Jen confirmed, her pulse racing all over again.

"Where did you find it?" Perry jumped in.

"It was found in the graveyard at St Francis near the entrance to the church," Judy said. "The officers are trying to locate the owners of the Fish & Chip Shop, My Plaice, to review their CCTV footage. They have a camera pointing towards the church," Judy explained.

14th December 11:05 Help

It was 11:05 a.m. now and their radio appeals were not help-ing. Some exaggerated leads claimed that they had seen Aoife in Scotland at 10:30 a.m. or that they'd seen a girl fitting that description get in a car at Asda's in Devon at 7:30 a.m. The officers were looking into all leads. "She can't have simply disappeared, she can't…" Jen said. "How can a six-year-old girl simply vanish?" None of them could answer and none of them tried.

"They're doing everything they can out there, I promise, no stone will be left unturned." Looking at Jen and Perry's faces, Judy wished she had chosen different words.

Perry said, "I can't sit here, I want to help." He headed for the door but Judy stood in his way. "Please, Perry, wait for the liaison officer. When Aoife comes home, she will need you both."

14th December 11:10
The Night Before

Judy sat them down, and once again asked them about the events of the night before. Jen had gone to bed at 11 pm, kissed the children goodnight, picked up the washing and put it in the laundry basket. "Aoife was wearing her unicorn jumper. Why didn't I think of that before? She went to bed early, about 7:00, she was tired, she said. We were a little surprised but she does do that sometimes, takes herself off when the day has been a bit overstimulating and, well, it's not unusual for her to sleep in her clothes. She doesn't like anything that scratches, you see, the labels are worst and she often wears her clothes inside out so the seams don't rub. Getting her in to her school uniform, well…" Jen stopped realising she was about to go off on a tangent it wasn't relevant to now.

"Thank you, Jen," Judy made more notes. Perry explained he had gone to bed around midnight. He had kissed Aoife goodnight closing the door behind him. "I didn't see what Aoife was wearing, I could just make out her face as the duvet was pulled up under her chin. I then checked in on Aubrey. Spark, his green dragon, was face down on the floor so I picked him up and placed him next to Aubrey. We've woken to the howls of Aubrey when Spark isn't beside him before." Perry stopped for a moment, remembering the first time that happened and how they thought something awful was up. Jen holding him wondering if they needed to call a doctor as Aubrey was too young to tell them what was on his mind. It was just pure chance that Perry put the dragon in the cot and Aubrey immediately stopped. Afterwards, all that could be heard was the catching of his breath as he recovered from his sobbing.

"I then kissed him goodnight and closed the door behind me," Perry explained.

"Thank you both, that's really helpful," Judy replied, putting her notebook in her pocket.

Interrupting the momentary silence, Perry offered, "Before going to bed, I make sure the windows and doors are locked." He paused a moment, stepping through the previous night's events in his mind, "I locked the backdoor as I always do and placed the key in there," pointing to the dish which held all of their household keys.

"Do you have an alarm system?" Judy asked.

"No," Jen and Perry responded in unison. And equally in unison hung their heads. It was another job they had put off until tomorrow. There were many tomorrow jobs on their list.

Perry was aware with each passing moment that Jen and he were starring in their own nightmare. It was hard to believe that when he woke, all that was on his mind was a board meeting…profit and loss, sales forecasts, striving for the dollar, spreadsheets and power points. It made him angry to think how skewed his priorities have been.

14th December Aoife

Aoife could feel the warmth from Gingerbread. It was no longer dark, "Oh no, I've been here too long, I have to go. I need to find Father Christmas."

Gingerbread sat up, ears pricked hanging on her every word. "Come on, Gingerbread, come on."

Unlike before, Gingerbread didn't sniff his way around the barn, he simply licked Aoife and jumped off the bale. Aoife grabbed her boots, they slid perfectly over her thick Christmas socks and they were dry and soft. Grabbing her coat, she closed it over her two jumpers and zipped it up. "Look," she said, beaming at Gingerbread, "I couldn't do that earlier."

The rip in her coat was also fixed, perhaps she'd imagined it. She picked up Stick and headed out of the barn.

Before she had fallen asleep, she knew the North Star was behind the barn so that's where Aoife headed with Gingerbread leading the way. She needed to hurry so that she could get back with the Christmas Spirit in time for dinner.

14th December 12:00
The Family and Liaison Officer

The bell rang. Jen and Perry had been in the house, suffocating in their not knowing while reporters multiplied outside. When the bell rang again, Jen and Perry stared at it and Judy answered.

In front of her stood a middle-aged man and woman. "We're Jeanne and Fred, Jen's parents," Jeanne offered, pointing at Fred and herself in case Judy was under any illusion that she meant somebody else. Judy looked at Jen who nodded and she let the couple pass.

Close behind them was a woman dressed in an oversized brown coat, hair a little windswept and her glasses balancing on the tip of her nose. Holding up her lanyard with her ID, she stated, "Emelda Hirst, family liaison." Judy allowed her to pass before closing the door on the circus outside.

Shaking Jen and Perry's hand, Jen couldn't help thinking how the name seemed a little old fashioned for a woman she suspected was no older than early 30s.

Jeanne headed straight for the kitchen. "I'll make some tea," she announced and negotiated her way around the kitchen expertly.

Jen watched for a moment while her mother pulled out cups and teabags while Fred dutifully filled the kettle on Jeanne's instruction.

In Jen's mind, time seemed to have rewound. She was catapulted back to another time when she had brought Aoife home and had sat in the very spot she was now holding her new born baby, while her mother instinctively knew what to do to comfort her. And that first cup of tea six and a half years

59

ago had tasted like home and safety. She raised a finger to her lips and rubbed gently across them, remembering the flavour of that 'builder's cuppa', as her dad called it.

"Two sugars please," Emelda responded. The sound of Emelda's voice snapped Jen back in to the present. On the table, she saw a picture of Aoife, the one that had hung in the corridor on the wall. She looked at Perry, perplexed how it had got there. Perry was looking at Emelda.

They'd had such a good day that day. They had all gone to the theme park and Aoife had laughed so much, she said, "Mummy, my tummy is going to burst." Jen clutched her waist.

It was all Jen could do not to scream. She could feel its momentum gathering pace.

Screaming would help no one, screaming had helped no one. Think! Think! Jen did nothing but think, that's why her stories, her plots, her 'tie-them-up-in-knots' novels were so good. And yet here, here and now, nothing. Ripped fabric on a fence and a unicorn bottle, their only clues. She looked down and opened her hands. The fabric was still clasped tightly in her right palm. Perry's hand was resting on her leg but she couldn't feel his touch. It was as if the fabric upon her skin was impenetrable—armoured. She was still piecing together every second of every minute of every hour and yet, she still couldn't understand why her little girl had left.

"Aoife, where have you gone…Aoife?" she had spoken aloud, the tears racing down her cheek; the dam had burst. Emelda reached for a pack of tissues in her pocket.

"Perry…" Jen looked at him, pleading with him to make it all stop. She couldn't join the dots, she couldn't join anything and two and two didn't make four, Aoife was not in the hut.

Jeanne gave her daughter a hug and kissed her on the forehead while Fred stood awkwardly waiting for instruction, a role he had taken on gladly over the years. But watching his daughter, seeing the pain and trying to manage his own, left him feeling inadequate—superfluous.

Jen didn't know that Perry kissed the kids goodnight every night other than when they went to bed together. She had never given it any thought. She should know though, shouldn't she? What had happened to them?

Fred brought the teas over and placed them on the table.

"Jen, can you tell me a little about Aoife? What did she like doing?" Emelda asked.

Emelda used the same questioning for Jen as she had for Perry, ensuring empathy due to this mother's increasing distress. She hated this job at times. Emelda's skill area, her speciality, was not liaising with families of missing children but assessing evidence and removing abused children from their families.

Emelda's instinct and intuition knew there was nothing sinister at the Mercier's household, but it was important to rule it out with evidence.

The call had come in at 9:00 a.m. giving her four hours of sleep, give or take a minute.

In the embrace of her taxi, she closed her eyes so that the jolly driver playing his Christmas songs wouldn't engage.

"34 Burgundy Road," she said as she climbed in to the back.

As it pulled up outside the address, hungry photographers snapped away while somebody thrust a microphone and a TV camera at her. She raised her hand and covered her face.

Perry watched his wife. Her beautiful fair skin had turned ashen, her eyes quizzical searching for answers.

"She loves to play hide and seek," Jen responded. Emelda wrote a note in her book and drew a line to corroborate Perry's words.

"She also loves to paint. She's actually pretty good," Jen said with a smile on her face. Jen pulled the piece of scrunched up paper out of her pocket and smoothed it out. "Look," she said, offering it to Emelda.

"That's pretty impressive," Emelda responded. "I struggle drawing the curtains."

The joke hung in the air and was met only with a chuckle from Fred. One look from Jeanne told him he had been inappropriate. He raised his eyebrows and sat on the single chair near the back door.

He listened for a minute as Emelda posed more questions before getting up and making his way to the bottom of the garden. He had heard all about the fence and how Aoife must have left the house and garden, and he couldn't help thinking he must fix it. If they had told him, he could have fixed it and then...he didn't finish his thought. Instead, he peaked through the child-size gap staring into the beyond and the grass covered in frost. The temperature was about 3 degrees, but last night it had dropped to -1. He couldn't allow himself to think too hard about whether she was warm enough, he just wanted to give her a grandad hug.

14th December 13:00
Reality Hits

Tom stood in the hall of the Mercier residence with two colleagues. Perry noticed how Judy seemed to know them both. Judy had remained a constant in the house since showing up with Aoife's bottle. Occasionally, she would be on the radio talking with her colleagues but generally, she just sat in the background observing.

She came over to say goodbye and to introduce her colleague PC Rearden. "Bella will do," the PC offered, shaking Perry's hand. Jen was at the bottom of the garden, her mother keeping a watchful but distant eye from the house and Perry stood next to the breakfast bar. His phone was continuously pinging one email after another and a message from Gary which he would respond to later. *Did it need a response?* he wondered. The message said, *"Let me know if there is anything I can do."* There wasn't and again, the feeling of helplessness rose in him.

He had still not been able to contact his parents who had taken a cruise. His mother's old Nokia phone kept going to voice and it was not the kind of message he would like to record.

Tom had been speaking with Emelda and both were heading in Perry's direction. Perry instinctively walked towards them, "Do you have news?"

"No, I'm afraid not, Perry," Tom responded and then proceeded, "These hours are crucial and I would like to put out an appeal…a nationwide television appeal to see if the public can help." Perry felt as though he'd been hit in the face and punched in the stomach, and that familiar sickness rose. In among all of the surrealism, there was hope that the next knock on the door would be Aoife with a somebody or other; there was hope that the next ping, the next call would be somebody announcing they had found her safe. There was still the hope that she would jump out of a cupboard or from behind the sofa.

But now this, this was big. This was a declaration that there were no significant leads. He had seen these appeals before, he had watched the devastation on other families' faces, wondering what he would do, then not wondering as the trauma would be too great as he switched over the TV for lighter entertainment.

Yet here he was and there they were. "Perry, we believe this to be important and you and Jen…" Perry didn't let them finish. He spoke to Jeanne and she headed to the bottom of the garden to bring Jen up.

Tom's phone rang, "Okay, get it back to the station as soon as you can." One of his team had located the owner of My Plaice. He was in Leeds visiting his daughter at a university and was now on the fast train back. They expected to receive the video footage within the next two and a half hours.

14th December 15:00
Jeanne Taylor

Jeanne Taylor arrived home at 14:30. She walked into her kitchen, put on the kettle and made herself cheese on toast, grilled, the way she preferred it. She then proceeded to remove her heels and slid in to her moccasin slippers. "Ahh, that's better," she said to herself.

She switched on the TV and sat down with her tray. As she always did, she flicked channels, Christmas movies galore on many of them but she didn't feel like watching another repeat. So, she kept it where it was while taking a bite of her toast and a sip of tea, and thought about her day.

She'd been thinking about the interview. She could never gauge whether anybody liked her or wanted her these days. At 58, she felt like she was already out to pasture and all she wanted was a little job to get her out of the house, keep her mind busy and her body active.

When she had seen the job advertisement at the garden centre in the next town, she applied with no expectation whatsoever. Jeanne had found that she could get in front of the interviewer but over the past six months, her efforts had not amounted to an offer. But she continued to hold on to optimism.

She was thinking about this as the news came on. Jeanne went to pick up the remote to switch over and knocked it on to the floor. She preferred to block out the agonising state of the world. A 'tut' escaped her lips as the remote hit the ground and she decided to eat first and hop around the channels again afterwards.

Noting the time on her very old grandfather clock, which stood proud next to her TV, she wondered exactly where the day had gone.

On the TV, a couple, Jen and Perry Mercier, were sat behind a long table. In front of them were microphones and beside them Inspector Tom Johnson who was talking now.

The penny was dropping. She knew the couple; she had known them since primary school. She had been a dinner lady then, many years ago, almost 30 years ago in fact. She listened, her hand over her mouth and a tear rolling down her cheek as they spoke of their missing child. A photo of Aoife, their daughter, was behind them on the screen with beautiful auburn hair, chocolate skin and the most beautiful freckles.

Perry had the same auburn hair but his was curly and he always kept it short. *Such a shame,* Jeanne found herself thinking. Aoife's smile revealed missing front teeth. She looked happy. *She looks like an angel,* Jeanne thought.

"If anybody has seen or heard anything, please contact the police," Jen uttered, her voice steady and tears streaming down her cheeks. Then looking straight down the camera lens, Jen said, "Aoife, pumpkin, if you're watching, please come home, we love you very much."

The camera cut to the inspector as Jen disappeared into the fold of her husband, the distress evident by the shaking of her body. An emergency contact number flashed up on the TV. "Oh my, how heart-breaking," Jeanne sighed.

Jeanne lost her appetite and placed the toast in the food bin and poured the remaining tea down the sink.

14th December Aoife

Aoife had walked a long way but she wasn't tired at all. She knew she was getting closer to Father Christmas. The snow was becoming thicker underfoot and she could smell hot chocolate, cookies and gingerbread.

She looked at her furry friend and laughed because in spite of his name, he didn't smell anything like a gingerbread, in fact, he smelt a bit windy and Aoife wrinkled her nose at the thought of it.

Aoife missed her mummy but knew when she returned home, the Christmas Spirit would make her happy again.

It had become a little darker and the North Star winked at her in the sky, "Look, Gingerbread, can you see? I think we're nearly there." Gingerbread came bounding back, his bell jingling louder and louder as he approached and fading as he ran off in to the distance.

Suddenly, Aoife stopped. "Gingerbread," she whispered. "Gingerbread, come here," Gingerbread started barking. "Shhh, Gingerbread, you'll scare it." There in front of them was a reindeer with large antlers and it was staring right at Aoife.

Aoife was steadfast. Lifting its right leg, the deer tapped on the ground and nodded its head. Aoife had seen a black horse do that in a film she had watched. The deer began to grunt. Aoife thought for a moment, "Do you want me to come with you?"

The deer began moving towards the trees from where it had appeared then stopped, looking back at Aoife. Gingerbread was still barking. "Shhh, Gingerbread. Come here," she bent down and gave Gingerbread a hug and began walking slowly towards the deer.

For each step she took, the deer took one step forward. It began to snow, so Aoife pulled up her hood and Gingerbread jumped on all fours trying to eat the falling flakes. Aoife then stopped, remembering why she was on this journey and asked, "Will you take me to see Father Christmas?"

The deer stopped, lifted its head and, looking back at Aoife, it grunted. Aoife took this as a 'yes'. She beamed then she laughed, and Gingerbread didn't know what to do with this excitement, so he barked.

14th December 15:03
Miss Johnson

Jen had phoned ahead and Jeanne and Fred were waiting for Aubrey when Miss Johnson brought him out. Today, Miss Johnson's ice queen demeanour had melted, Jeanne noted as the nursery teacher escorted Aubrey to his grandparents.

Aubrey almost dropped Spark on his run up to Grandad. Fred held him for longer than he should have and Aubrey squeezed his grandad's soft, sagging cheeks while assessing his demeanour. Fred quickly adjusted his frown.

"Where Mummy?" Aubrey asked.

It was Jeanne that spoke, "She's popped to the shops and will be back soon so she asked if we can come and get you."

"Where Fifi?"

Fred responded, "We'll see her later, munchkin, let's get you home."

Jeanne and Fred exchanged glances. Home, home was surrounded by reporters and photographers. "Change of plan, let's go somewhere fun," Jeanne said.

Aubrey was trying to read the situation and, in the end, leaned in to his grandad with one hand hanging down and Spark clasped in his palm.

Alicia Johnson walked back into the classroom replaying the conversation with her father earlier that day. He'd been an inspector for many years and had told her about Aoife being missing. She found herself watching Aubrey all day as if her presence alone would keep him safe from the potential devastation that may ensue—from the news he may have to endure. She didn't know what or when it may filter through the nursery door.

Alicia watched Aubrey, admiring his carefree nature as he threw the tatty, green dragon up in the air over and over, oblivious and uninterested in the children within the classroom.

She had asked Mrs Mercier over and again to please wean him off this comfort, but each drop off came attached to new reasoning why Spark accompanied Aubrey into class. Alicia worried as Aubrey wasn't making friends and his speech wasn't developing, it wasn't where it should be at three and a half years old.

As she packed away the paint and placed the books on the small shelves, her imagination and logical mind attempted to take her on a route she didn't want to consider and the weight of this sat heavy upon her.

She looked up and hoped her father and his force would find Aoife soon. He was the best in his field, that she knew; a man dedicated to his job. An absent father whom she used to blame and rebel against but as an adult, she found understanding and an affiliation for his quest for justice.

She came to believe everyone had their purpose. He was lucky he found his early. He had also found another partner, Izzy, the complete antithesis of her father.

Izzy was a jolly paramedic who coped with her demons through humour and both approached their relationship with an understanding that late nights were inevitable as were times of separation.

In turn, Alicia became a big sister to twins Jeffrey and Jonas, physically mirror images, but chalk and cheese in personality. She enjoyed her new responsibility, her role as their big sister. She missed them. Both had chosen universities away from home; one a whizz with computers and the other, a drama student.

Putting on her woollen hat, her oversized padded coat and her gloves and, locking the nursery door, she noticed how grey it was, the moon already visible in the sky.

14th December 15:05
Jeanne Taylor

Jeanne had kept the TV on in the background, she heard the news reporter announce the breaking news as she cut to video footage and a senior police officer.

Aoife was seen on CCTV with a dog heading away from St Francis Church. Through the voices was a jingling of a bell and Jeanne was transported back to the early hours: the sight of a dog, a jingle of a bell and a girl's voice shouting 'Gingerbread'.

"The dog," the officer was saying, "is a Border Terrier cross by the name of Toby, he has a blue collar and a bell…" the officer began.

"The bell, I heard the bell. How could I forget?" Jeanne dropped the dishes. Jeanne ran downstairs and knocked on her neighbour's door. Jim answered. "Are the girls here, your grandchildren?"

"Hello, Jeanne," Jim responded, "No, they're coming next week, why?"

Jeanne, forgetting all manners, raced back up the stairs to her flat and searched for the number, flicking the channel to see if she could still catch it on the news.

"Hello…The dog, I saw the dog this morning. I…" Jeanne raced on.

"Slow down please, ma'am, can I take your name?" the voice at the other end asked.

Jeanne told the officer all about the morning's events, how she had been woken in the early hours, "I'm a light sleeper, you see," she said, "ever since my Philipp…" the officer steered her back, mindful that too many hours had passed. "It was the bell, you see, the sound of the bell on the TV that made me think, but the girl's voice was shouting 'Gingerbread' and they said the dog's name was Toby. I am so sorry, I thought it was Jinny and Jim's grandchildren but they're not here. Jim said they're not coming until next week."

"Okay, ma'am, an officer is on her way around, please stay where you are." And the line went dead.

The search party were at the other end of town. They had turned right when they reached Dalton Road.

Jeanne couldn't wait, she walked up and down, wearing out the floor of her small living room. *That poor girl had been missing since the early hours, she would be cold, frozen.* She grabbed her coat and scarf, placing her phone and keys in each side pocket and headed out.

Jinny was at the window watching her neighbour negotiate the traffic and race down Mill Hill Farm Road. A car screeched to a halt. She called Jim, "She's behaving very strangely, don't you think?"

"Ummm," was about all Jim could offer as he picked up his paper again, turning to the sports page and torturing himself with the team results.

A few minutes later, PC Judy Vincent was standing at number 25 Dalton Road. Receiving no reply after ringing the bell, Judy banged on the door and radioed back to confirm the address.

The bell rang at 27 Dalton Road and Jim answered the door to a young police officer. "I'm looking for Jeanne…Jeanne Taylor, your neighbour."

"Who is it, Jim?" Jinny hadn't seen this much traffic at her doorstep since the children were teenagers.

"It's a police officer looking for Jeanne!" Jim shouted behind him.

"Jinny, my wife, and I saw her racing down Mill Hill Farm Road about five minutes ago," Jim pointed as he spoke.

"Thank you, sir," the PC replied, "You've been a great help."

"What's going on? Is she in trouble?" Jim asked.

"No, sir," is all Judy offered as she negotiated the busy traffic.

14th December Aoife

Aoife looked up, she could barely see a thing through the snow that was falling fast and the ice-cold wind was blowing in her face. She lifted her scarf above her mouth, she could barely see Gingerbread, only hearing the sound of his bell. As she walked through the trees, she saw a vast open space.

The deer had stopped in its tracks. "Where's Father Christmas?"

She wanted to cry, she needed to get home, she was so very hungry and now her legs were aching and she was so cold, beginning to feel very tired; she wasn't sure whether she could walk much further.

The deer stared at Aoife for a little while then lay down close by, swinging its head onto its side and grunting. A little afraid, Aoife watched for a moment.

The deer appeared to be willing her to climb on.

Gingerbread was running around the deer in a circle, barking so loud that Aoife couldn't think. She took one step closer to the deer and when it didn't move, she took another, until she was able to put her hand on its back and stroke it.

Gingerbread's barking was accompanied by the bell and neither sounds were soothing Aoife right now. "Shhh, Gingerbread, please, I can't think." Gingerbread stopped beside Aoife and she bent over and hugged him.

She lifted a leg over the deer and sat on its back. She then realised that she was no longer holding Stick. She looked around, nothing but soft, white snow, and she slipped off the deer retracing her steps. There in the virgin snow, she saw a brown imprint. "Stick!" she announced as if being reunited with a long-lost friend.

Slowly, she approached the deer climbing onto his back. The deer began to rise. "Stop!" she shouted. "Gingerbread...I have to pick up Gingerbread, he's tired too, please." The deer swung its head around as if seeing them for the first time, Aoife marvelled at the size of its antlers. One eye on Aoife, the deer bent a knee and bowed. "Come on, Gingerbread, jump."

Gingerbread jumped around and around in circles but didn't jump up. "Gingerbread, please, I have to go. Jump, it's okay, I'll look after you." After a few more twirls, Gingerbread stopped, looked, backed up and ran up so that he could make the leap.

Aoife grabbed the little dog and pulled him close. She couldn't imagine this journey without her companion now.

The deer trotted and then speeded up. Aoife put her head down and held on to it, one arm firmly around its neck, as the other held on to Gingerbread.

Before she knew it, they were in the air flying above the trees. Looking down, their crowns were quickly disappearing.

Excitement and disbelief raced around her tummy. They hadn't been in the air long when the snow stopped and a bright light filled the sky, warming her cheeks and thawing her hands.

She looked up, and in the distance she could see a house...no, houses. Gingerbread was barking again. "Shhhh, it's okay," Aoife said, "we're going to meet Father Christmas." The deer landed on a bright green stretch of grass and lay down.

Gingerbread jumped off first and Aoife slid landing on her side while she waited for her aching legs to wake up.

She sat brushing her gloved hands across the grass. In the distance was a house with smoke coming out of the chimney and she could smell hot chocolate again.

The smell was enticing her towards the gingerbread house in front of them.

She looked around.

"Thank you, deer," Aoife said as it trotted off towards its friends.

"Is that…?" she clasped her hand over her mouth, in case her excitement burst out, as she spotted a deer with a bright nose by a barn.

Somebody was calling her name. In front of her, a girl with pointy ears about the size of Aoife.

Was she an elf? Aoife thought, a smile of apprehension and happiness forming all at once.

Gingerbread barked. "Oh, Gingerbread, you're such a scaredy-cat," Aoife giggled as all of her fears had left her.

The elf held out her hand and offered Gingerbread a biscuit. All at once, Gingerbread's fear also left as he wagged his tail and his bottom joined in the display.

"You're very welcome here, Gingerbread, don't be afraid," the elf said.

Aoife wondered how she knew Gingerbread's name but then thought, *Of course, I just said it.* Then her cheeks flushed a little even though the elf couldn't hear Aoife's thoughts.

"Let's get you inside," she said to Aoife, extending an arm to lift her from the grass. "We've been expecting you and you must be very hungry by now; you've been out for such a long time."

Aoife was excited, she managed to get her aching legs upright and followed the elf towards the big gingerbread house.

The smoke from the chimney smelt of gingerbread and something else. *Mummy's candles,* she thought and just for a moment, her smile slipped. Inside the house was a roaring fire taller than Aoife, *and nearly as wide as her bedroom*, she thought. The flames danced—red, yellow and blue. Next to the fire, a large chair with a big soft cushion.

"Make yourself at home," the elf offered as she walked towards the kitchen where a lady as tall as her mummy with the same coloured hair was standing with an apron strapped around her waist and flour on her nose.

She walked over and gave Aoife a hug, "Welcome, Aoife," and looking down at Gingerbread, "and you too, Gingerbread."

Aoife wondered how they knew to expect them and as she did, the lady lifted her up onto the big chair, then Gingerbread took a run up, jumped and sat beside her before eventually lying on her lap.

"How was the journey?" the lady, which by now Aoife had deduced was Mrs Christmas, asked. She decided this as she looked very much like a picture Aoife had drawn in her sketchbook and then the next sentence confirmed it, and Aoife was very pleased with herself for guessing it right. Even though nobody was joining in her game.

"My husband will be along shortly, he's just in the office organising the elves. There are so many toys to make before Christmas Eve."

Aoife's hands and feet tingled as they began to thaw. As feeling returned, she stripped her coat off revealing her snowman jumper.

"Ahhh, lovely," Mrs Christmas said. "You're wearing your Christmas jumper. Father Christmas will be so pleased. He knew you'd like it."

Aoife beamed, her cheeks hurt from how broad it was and her heart was happy.

"You know," she continued, "he can remember every single present he gifted any child." Aoife offered no response, she just listened while looking around.

The furniture was red and so soft and the arms had green fabric draped across them. The coffee table had a large candle in the middle and a small wooden Santa on a bike. The only light in the room came from the fire and the small windows in the gingerbread walls.

Aoife absorbed it all, and as she did she relaxed in to the safety of her surroundings, sinking in to the chair that was large enough for her whole family, she felt.

"Oh, how rude of me, I haven't even introduced myself. I'm Peggy Christmas. Father Christmas is my husband but I think I told you that already," and she released a, "Ha, Ha, Ha. I'd forget my head if it wasn't screwed on. Ha, Ha, Ha." And Peggy's chest rose with each chuckle and her head tilted back. *Just like when Father Christmas laughs,* Aoife thought as Peggy Christmas made her way to the kitchen, heels clicking.

She returned, placing a large cup of hot chocolate with marshmallows on top of a table beside the chair, and she sprinkled a little bit of cinnamon and a lot of chocolate sprinkles over the top as she winked at Aoife as if they'd shared an unspoken, 'I won't tell if you don't,' between them. "There, that'll warm you up deep inside…get those cold bones defrosted."

She then handed Aoife a cookie and Gingerbread a biscuit shaped like a bone. Gingerbread raised his head but didn't eat it. He simply closed his eyes again and continued to sleep.

Just as Aoife was about to take a bite, the door opened and a large figure dressed in red filled the space. As he stepped inside, Aoife forgot she was hungry and she also forgot to breathe.

"Now, who do we have here?" Father Christmas asked. "No, don't tell me," and he laughed, "Ho ho ho," his shoulders rose up then down, his chest and large belly joined in, synchronising.

"Aoife, I presume?"

Aoife was still struggling to get a word out. "Yes" escaped barely audible.

"Well, Aoife, I'm really pleased to finally meet you. I know you are on an important mission, so how can I help you?" Aoife thought how Father Christmas looked just like the picture she had painted, the one she had hated and thrown in her bin. She would take it out again when she got home, she promised herself.

Aoife began to tell Father Christmas all about her quest to find the Christmas spirit and how that would make Mummy smile again and then they could buy a tree. "I really love Christmas trees," Aoife found herself saying, "and we always have one, a really big one that almost hits the ceiling and Daddy always lifts me up to put the angel on top and then we all watch as the lights go on, and Daddy always forgets to check so sometimes we have to take them all off again, then Mummy makes those eyes where her eyebrows go up," Aoife demonstrated, "and she winks at me and sometimes Daddy has to get new lights cause emmm…he isn't very good at fixing things and Mummy always gives him a kiss when he gets cross with himself, and then he pretends to be cross with Mummy because she's always right and Daddy whispers, 'Don't encourage her,' and I laugh, and Aubrey jumps around with Spark," Aoife stopped out of breath, feeling a bit sad. She missed her mummy and daddy and she missed Aubrey and his green dragon.

Peggy Christmas and Father Christmas were both perched on the big red sofa hanging on Aoife's every word. "Oh, my…" Peggy said. Aoife was now crying. Gingerbread sat up and began licking her face.

"Well, that settles it then," Father Christmas said as he stood up. Aoife's eyes followed him.

Peggy walked over to the little girl, brushed her auburn hair back and said, "Drink up, dear, it'll be okay." When Aoife picked up her hot chocolate, it was merely warm, she ate each soggy marshmallow individually, then swallowed the tastiest drink she had ever had and nibbled on her chocolate cookie while Gingerbread, now awake and attentive, woofed down his biscuit, sniffing about the chair for the remaining crumbs.

Aoife didn't remember falling asleep but when she woke, Father Christmas was sat opposite.

"Better?" he asked.

"Yes," Aoife nodded.

"Would you like to see the workshop?" he asked.

Aoife nodded so vigorously, her head might have dropped off. "Come on, Gingerbread," she said as she gently encouraged him off her lap.

Father Christmas grabbed both of her hands and lowered her onto the red rug. Holding on to Father Christmas' hand, Aoife walked outside down the path away from the gingerbread house.

It was very bright; it made her eyes a little sore and Aoife wished she'd brought her sunglasses.

She placed a hand over her brow like a visor and walked on with Father Christmas.

Crossing the snowfield, she could still see the reindeer. She looked over.

Father Christmas followed her gaze. "I knew he would be just the deer to get you here safely," he said.

Aoife smiled at the dashing reindeer who had brought her here, and his friends who were grazing beside him. The stag responded by looking up, tapping his hoof and bowing.

In the background, she could hear noise a bit like the steam engine sound when Nana and Grandad McKenzie had taken her to Cockrow Railway. With each step, the noise grew louder.

"Don't mind that," Father Christmas said, acknowledging the quizzical look upon her face. "That's the workshop. A lot of machines work around the clock to get the toys ready for the boys and girls."

Leaning down so that he was at her level, he said, "Would you like to help?" Aoife nodded and Father Christmas gave her a thumbs up. They were greeted at the door by the same elf that had brought Aoife and Gingerbread to the house. "Hello, Steen," Father Christmas said.

" Hello, Nicholas. Hello, Aoife, come on in."

Gingerbread wasn't allowed in to the workshop so Aoife watched as he was led off outside. She could still hear him barking as the door closed. "Don't worry, Aoife, he'll be getting some nice food and drink ready for when you go home," Father Christmas said as he handed her some earmuffs.

The workshop was very busy, she wanted to see it all but there were elves everywhere and toys stacked high, and so much noise even with the muffs covering her ears.

She recognised a bike that she had when she was four, it had three wheels and was blue. She hadn't wanted the pink one, her favourite colour was blue.

There on the conveyor belt were teddies, lots of them that looked just like Aubrey's. Everyone was running around very excited and Aoife's head was whirling. She pulled on Father Christmas's sleeve.

"Okay, Aoife," and suddenly they were outside. "It's time to get you home, Aoife. That's enough excitement for today," Father Christmas said.

"But the Christmas Spirit? I need to take the Christmas Spirit," Father Christmas placed his hand gently upon her head and said, "Trust me, it will be there…"

"But," Aoife interrupted.

Father Christmas squatted in front of her, "Aoife, have I ever let you down?" Aoife did think about it and decided no, he had always kept his promise even when she asked him to bring Mummy the necklace she had seen in the shop window in town and even when Aubrey had wanted that train set which Daddy said was no longer in the shops. Father Christmas had always kept his promise. So, she looked at Father Christmas and shook her head.

"It's time to go home now," Father Christmas said. Aoife nodded; she was very tired.

"What does she look like? The Christmas Spirit, what does she look like?" Aoife asked.

Father Christmas smiled at Aoife and all at once, she felt warm inside. "Aoife, the Christmas Spirit is something that lives within you, within me, within children and within adults the world over. It has no colour, no creed, it has no shape or form, it has no single song and no solitary scent, and you cannot touch it or hold it within your arms. The Christmas Spirit is different for everyone. You will know when you have found it because you will feel the emotion of it, you will sing the song that most celebrates it, you will smell that scent that makes you know it's in your home. You will know that it has arrived, as it will touch you here." Father Christmas put his hand over his heart before lifting Aoife's and placing it on hers. For a moment, neither said anything at all. Aoife's young mind whirled with thoughts and questions. But which thought or question should she ask first? Even when a thought or question popped into her mind and rushed to her lips, it was quickly replaced by another thought or question that seemed more important than the last, as she pondered on Father Christmas's words. In the end she asked nothing and processed plenty. One thing she had learned, the Christmas Spirit lived, but not as she had imagined.

The stag was making his way towards them closely followed by Gingerbread who, apart from jingling, wasn't making any noise at all.

Peggy came out of her gingerbread house and gave them both a big hug.

She then zipped up Aoife's coat, pulled up her hat and wrapped her scarf around her neck. "Now, there you go, that'll keep you warm. You take good care. You'll be home in no time at all. This, the dearest and wisest of our reindeers, has strict instructions to take you straight to the front door," Peggy told her.

"Thank you for visiting us," she continued before kissing Aoife's cheek and returning to the warmth of her gingerbread house.

Father Christmas lifted Aoife onto the reindeers' back and then he picked up Gingerbread who snuggled up against Aoife. This time, the stag wore reins and a saddle. Aoife fed the reins through her right hand, the way Father Christmas showed her, and wrapped her left arm under Gingerbread while gripping the saddle. "Comfortable?" Father Christmas asked. Aoife nodded, not wanting to speak as she swallowed down the sadness she felt about leaving.

Looking at the deer Father Christmas ordered, "My faithful friend make sure you get Aoife home safely,", and he gently stroked the reindeer's neck. The stag grunted, tapping his hoof on the green stretch of grass.

"Goodbye, Aoife! Don't worry, all will be fine." He patted the deer on the rear and it raced down the green.

Aoife glanced back at Father Christmas who was waving and before she knew it, they were all caught up in the snowstorm once again. Aoife was shivering, Gingerbread pressed up against her so tightly and she held him close, one arm under his belly.

14th December 15:12
Jeanne Taylor

Jeanne Taylor rushed down Mill Hill Farm Road with an urgency she hadn't experienced for some time. "The last time was…" she chased that thought away.

Twelve hours had passed since her siting of the dog, since the girl shouted 'Gingerbread', since the jingle of the bell. Would she have put two and two together if they hadn't mentioned the bell? She chased the thought from her mind. She was here now.

At the end of Mill Hill Farm Road was Farmer Tully's field. The horses weren't out, the ground was frozen solid. There was no other way Aoife could have walked unless she had walked back up Mill Hill Farm Road when she reached the field.

There was no guarantee she and the dog were still together; they could have gone their separate ways. There were no guarantees about anything, she thought but she had to try.

From the edge of the field, she could see the barn. *Perhaps*…she began and abandoned her thought. She walked across the field, her boots slipping and her ankle tipping on solid ground. It took five minutes for her to reach the barn.

She looked inside. There was nothing to indicate life. She walked around hoping for clues. She stopped, there was a whimpering.

"Hello, anybody there? Hello!" this time much louder. The dog started barking and she followed the sound to a stack of bales behind another stack of bales. She bent over and peeked her head around. Pushed up against a corner, she could see the dog with its head resting on what looked to be a pile of clothes.

Jeanne climbed up, her legs creaking and a pain shooting down her back. She got closer and the dog barked louder but it didn't move. It was shivering. "Hello?" Jeanne moved slowly, "Toby, isn't it? I'm not going to hurt you." Toby whimpered. She approached the bale with caution, talking gently to the dog, her eyes fixated on what she now knew was probably the missing girl, Aoife. Toby stopped barking but remained in his spot.

As she got closer to the girl, she kneeled on an Ugg boot. It was soaking wet and the cold water seeped through her trousers and dampened her knees. With a little more urgency, she manoeuvred herself level with the girl's head in line with Toby who was still burrowing into Aoife's neck.

"Oh please, God." Once positioned, Jeanne curled herself around Aoife, unzipped her coat, pulled out her phone and lay it across them both. She felt for a pulse, it was weak but Jeanne breathed a sigh of relief and dialled 999.

"What's your emergency?"

" Aoife, I found the missing girl Aoife in the field in Mill Hill Farm Road…in the barn, in the…in the field, we're in the barn in the field. Please hurry, she's so cold."

"Madam, what's your name?" the operator enquired.

"Jeanne, Jeanne Taylor."

"Okay, Jeanne, I'm going to put you through to the ambulance service, they will need to ask you some questions. Okay? Jeanne, are you there?"

"Yes, sorry, I'm here, her pulse, it's very weak, she's so cold. She is breathing but it's very shallow," Jeanne continued.

"Jeanne, I need you to focus, the police are on their way. Please stay where you are." There was a break in the conversation then a click, and Jeanne was patched through to the ambulance service.

Judy was just recovering her balance from a slip on the ice down Mill Hill Farm Road when the call came in.

"Yes, sir, I'm almost there." She could see the barn in the distance and negotiated the field as quickly as she could.

"Hello! Hello, anybody here?" she shouted. Jeanne didn't respond. Judy followed the voice, "Was she singing?"

On the bale, she saw a dog and a woman hugging what looked like a pile of clothes. Judy climbed up and lifted the small dog up. It began to whimper, shivering in its coarse fur coat. She placed it on the floor and climbed onto the bale in front of Aoife, struggling to separate emotion from professionalism as she assessed.

Poor thing, she thought as she brushed Aoife's auburn hair from her face. The woman who Judy deduced was Jeanne Taylor was shivering, she had removed her coat and it was covering the little girl, while she lay pressed up against her, spooning.

Aoife's lips were blue and her skin ice-cold but there was a pulse. Judy let out an involuntary sigh of relief.

"The ambulance is on its way," Jeanne said without taking her eye off the little girl. "Aoife, Aoife, can you hear me?" Jeanne whispered in her ear. She stroked her hair and removing one of her gloves, rubbed her hand.

"Please don't do that," Judy intervened. "It's possible she has hypothermia and rubbing or massaging is not advisable. We just need to keep her warm until the ambulance arrives."

Jeanne was a little startled by the PC's abruptness and then equally mortified that she could have potentially exacerbated the situation. The sounds of sirens in the distance grew louder with every second and silence fell between the two women for just a moment as both allowed their own emotions to dissipate.

"I'm Jeanne, Jeanne Taylor."

"Judy Vincent," the PC offered.

Jeanne spoke, keeping her body pressed up against Aoife's to keep her warm. "I heard a little girl calling 'Gingerbread' this morning at around 3:20 a.m.…I thought…I thought it was my neighbours' grandchildren. They come over a lot, you see, they're seven and five, and sometimes they lead their grandparents a merry dance," she smiled as she recalled some of the antics those two children had been up to, "and our walls, well, they're not so thick. But then the TV, I don't normally watch the news, you see, it's very depressing, isn't it?" Jeanne said but took no break in her speech for Judy to respond as she continued, "The reporter or was it the police officer, I can't remember, they mentioned a dog, a dog with a bell, Toby, I think they said, and I remembered and knew then…if only I had realised. Oh God…what if?"

Silence fell, seemingly stretching for an eternity, but in reality seconds had barely passed when Judy responded a little softer than before, "The most important thing is you found Aoife." Judy then placed her hand on Jeanne's shoulder.

"Yes, yes of course, of course," Jeanne responded.

"Are you warm enough?" she asked Jeanne, lifting the shaking dog off the barn floor. Jeanne nodded, not wishing to complain and feeling she was in a much better way than the little girl she was pressed up against.

Sitting on a bale, Judy opened her coat and slipped Toby inside to warm him up.

The sirens were now upon them.

14th December 15:25 Tom

The unmarked police car pulled up outside the barn. Tom stepped out of the passenger side and Bella from the driver's side.

Negotiating its way up the field was the ambulance.

Tom entered the barn and Bella waved the ambulance in.

Tom spoke with Judy briefly before returning to the car for foil blankets.

Jeanne rose, feeling the bite of the cold as she separated from Aoife. She then lifted her coat off Aoife so that the inspector could place a foil blanket around her.

She looked so small, face and limbs barely visible at all. More like a pile of clothing on a bale, Tom thought as he watched, barely able to see any rise or fall to indicate life.

Jeanne placed her coat back over Aoife.

"Are you sure?" Tom said looking at Jeanne.

Jeanne nodded as she accepted the blanket Tom extended her. "She needs it more than me," Jeanne responded and she sat on the bale pulling Toby towards her, watching, observing, but not able to hear the whisperings between the officers.

14th December 15:30
Accident and Emergency

Emelda was at the bottom of the garden on the phone, "I understand, thank you. Yes, I'll let them know."

The bell rang, Perry answered. "Mr Mercier, is it true they've found Aoife, any comment?" The photographers were perched like gargoyles on the steps and were snapping away hungry for a shot.

"What? When? Is this some kind of joke?" Perry responded, as the woman thrust her voice recorder at him.

Damn, Emelda thought, as she raced to the door. She pushed it closed. "Perry, Jen, there has been a development."

Jen stood at Aoife's door consumed in thought. She'd been standing there since returning from their press conference earlier with nothing but thoughts racing around her mind. Fruitless, useless thoughts stirring up blame, looking and searching for signs, just some indication about where her little girl had gone and why. Jen's arms were folded around her waist clutching Aoife's picture of Father Christmas. "Perry," Emelda called, commanding but gentle all at once.

Perry was fixed to the spot, staring at the closed door, "What do they mean Aoife's been found?" his voice was raised.

Hearing Perry shout, Jen turned and approached his direction. "What's going on?" she asked, her eyes fixed on Emelda.

"Sit down, both of you, please!" Emelda asked, veering them towards the living room.

"What's happened?" Jen asked, her words more urgent.

Harjot had left his post for just a couple of minutes to use the bathroom and was now racing towards the door, apologising as he reached for the handle. The press swarmed like vultures, pushing and shoving their way to the door in a quest to be first to feast and splash distress or comfort across the tabloids or televisions. It mattered not which, as this story had now become a nationwide interest.

"Jen, Perry, any comment…how's Aoife?" somebody shouted through the door before it slammed shut, cutting off the deep dulcet tones of Harjot shouting.

"Step away from the property please, sir…sir! Madam, remove yourself…"

The house fell silent again for a moment. Jen and Perry sat on their red sofa, eyes fixated on Emelda. "Aoife has been found," Emelda confirmed.

Jen stood up, "Oh thank God, where? Where is she?"

"Is she…" Perry interrupted, frustration rising, "How do the press know?"

Emelda diverted her attention from Jen to Perry, "I've no idea, Perry, but Aoife was found in a barn on a farmer's field at the other end of town. An ambulance is with her now, we need to get you…"

Perry raced for the door before Emelda finished. "Tully's," he said.

It was Jen that stopped him, placing herself between him and the door. Holding his face, she said, "Perry, wait, listen…"

Emelda continued quickly, nodding at Jen, "We need to get you to the hospital. Aoife needs you both."

The fear slapped Perry in the face and he fell silent.

"Is she…is she?" Jen spoke but the words didn't quite hit the air and faded from a whisper into nothingness.

"She's alive…" Emelda began.

"Oh, thank God, thank God," Jen and Perry responded in unison.

"But I don't have any other news, I'm sorry, I've been asked to get you both to the hospital…St Peters."

There was a brief pause while Emelda gathered her thoughts. Pushing her glasses back on to the bridge of her nose, she said, "I suggest we leave through the back, through your neighbour's garden."

Jen nodded, grabbed her bag, coat and scarf and picked her phone off the coffee table on her way out. Perry followed, locking the backdoor behind them and picked his phone up dialling Dave's number. He had stopped looking at his phone hours earlier and as the screen burst into life at his touch, he noted 15 additional missed calls.

"Aubrey!" Jen stopped in her tracks and phoned her parents to give them the news. As Jen got closer, Perry could hear. "I have to go…Yes, St Peter's…I don't know, I really have to go. Yes, we'll see you there." Jen put the phone down. She was now alongside Perry walking through Dave and Laura's back garden. Dave patted Perry on the back in the absence of knowing what suitable words to use.

Emelda phoned the taxi firm and asked that it pull up at the corner of Burgundy Road and Cherry Lane with strict instructions that the driver was to call her once they'd arrived. "It's a delicate situation," was all Emelda offered to the receptionist. She had taken a name to ensure that it wasn't some reporter taking the opportunity. Emelda had seen a lot of stunts from hungry press in the past.

Lynn was asked to call Emelda's number once parked up. She reached Cherry Lane at 15:59. "Hello, it's Lynn…Lynn Sturgess, the taxi driver. I've pulled over in Cherry Lane. I'm in a white Corsa registration, R6."

"I'll find you," Emelda said, cutting Lynn off quite abruptly.

Emelda, Jen and Perry exited through Dave and Laura's side gate onto Cherry Lane. Perry and Jen climbed in to the back and Emelda sat next to the driver, nodding a silent hello as she strapped herself in. Lynn turned her car around, heading back down Cherry Lane towards the hospital. She recognised the couple in her rear-view mirror as Jen and Perry Mercier from their television appeal earlier. Lynn wanted to ask the burning question on everyone's lips but the atmosphere in the car was heavy with pain and her curiosity had no place within this space.

Perry's phone rang. "Perry, it's Mum, is everything okay? I've just switched on my phone and I've got two missed calls from you."

"Hi, Mum, yes everything's fine," Perry lied, swallowing the pain of the day's events. "Where are you?" he continued.

"Well, we've just arrived in the Caribbean. We're heading on to the beach and your dad's keen to get a few cocktails in. You okay? You don't sound great."

"It's a bit of a cold, that's all, I just had a memory lapse, forgot you were on your cruise and just wanted to see how you were. I'll speak to you when you get home," Perry lied some more, "Not too many cocktails now, we don't want you dancing on tables again."

His mother laughed and said, "I won't, you know that was 20 years ago and I wish your dad had never told you that story. Speak soon, Son. I love you, give my love to the children and Jen."

"I love you too, Mum. Bye."

As he put the phone down, he swallowed hard, he turned his head away from his wife and fought the tears. Not now, he couldn't break now, his little girl would need him strong. Jen was staring at him. "They're too far away…well, we don't know ourselves…" he offered up to her silence.

"It's okay," Jen said, "I get it," and she squeezed his hand.

"Aoife, well, she is in the best place now. I just wish we knew…she'll be fine, won't she?" Perry stumbled over every word as he searched Jen's face hoping for clues, hoping that her insight and intuition would be on high alert so that he could use that to summon the strength to suppress anguish and turmoil within. Jen squeezed his hand again. He didn't want to think of the worst in case he invited that terrible possibility in. Jen often told him, *Be careful what you put in to the universe,* he thought. So, he was careful, more careful than he had ever been. He didn't really believe all of that karma stuff and the universe giving back, but today, he would believe in fairies, unicorns and the universe if that is what was needed to bring Aoife home safe.

They were outside St Peter's Hospital within 25 minutes.

The press was camped outside A&E primed to pounce. Emelda took the lead while Jen and Perry kept their heads down as they raced through the entrance.

Inside, they were met by the inspector. Tom respectfully but firmly encouraged the press to stay outside and allow Jen and Perry their privacy.

The corridor stretched ahead of them for an eternity, it felt to Jen. Her legs were unsteady. It felt the only thing keeping her upright were fatigued muscles and they would give way at any moment, she was certain of that.

Stop it! Stop it now Jenna Mercier, she motioned. *Aoife needs you strong.* She reminded herself. Shaking that negativity from her mind, she chased the thoughts of doom away replacing them with determination. *She's not going to...we won't need a miracle just the strength and the might of Aoife's will.*

Jen was certain Aoife possessed both of those qualities in abundance. She chastised herself for going to such a dark place and snapped back in to the present.

Perry disliked everything about hospitals. He had since childhood; he wretched at the smell, the lighting made him dizzy, his own feelings of mortality made him fear and the memory of his grandfather dying so quickly still caused him nightmares.

It was a lifetime ago. He was a ten-year-old boy in and out of hospital for 11 long days and nights, straight from the school gate and all through the weekend. Homework took place in the corridors or the hospital family room, while his mother cared for her rapidly deteriorating father and his dad chased sales up and down the UK.

Perry had lived in Weybridge at that time and soon after their loss, his mother orchestrated a move or, as he now referred to it, ran from her pain and her grief, and they settled in Cambridge in the middle of year five. In a matter of 30 days, he had lost his grandfather, buried him and left behind the only life and friends he had known.

Four years later, after seeing a psychologist, his mother apologised for not being more empathic towards him and his loss. She had been diagnosed with Post Traumatic Stress Disorder and only after she completed that healing process did they begin to live their life.

Here he was again in that same hospital, beads of sweat upon his brow and his hands clammy with anticipation of what he would find—what they would be told. He looked over at his wife and noticed for the first time that she was squeezing his hand.

Suddenly, there they stood outside Aoife's room and Tom was saying something.

14th December 15:23
First Respondent

Izzy was the first respondent to the call and she and Jerome raced through the traffic, turning left off Dalton Road. The icy surface on Mill Hill Farm Road forced Izzy to slow the ambulance right down as the gathering crowd at the end of it were causing an obstruction. It never failed to amaze Izzy how many times they had to encourage the public to move out of the way. It was, at times, as if they were selling ice cream rather than the sirens warning of an emergency. With a beeping of their horn, the crowd began to disburse, leaving just enough room for the ambulance to squeeze through the gap they'd forged. Quickly the crowd closed the gap again as curiosity and concern, for a girl they did not know, won them over.

Jerome pointed, "Over there, Izzy, I can see a copper waving." Izzy nodded and drove carefully towards the officer.

Both paramedics raced to the rear of their ambulance and pulled out their bags and noting the ice scattered across the grass like shards of glass, they both grabbed for the stretcher rather than the trolley.

In the barn, Izzy could hear Tom before she saw him. He was talking to a police officer whom she recognised as Judy and a woman who had a blanket wrapped around her. Izzy and Jerome were upon them in no time and all three adults parted the way so that they could reach the little girl. Tom and Izzy glanced at one another but no words passed between them. It was Judy who began filling them in on as much detail as she could about the events of the past 12 minutes since she arrived at the barn. The paramedics took Aoife's pulse and

Izzy called her name gently over and again, but Aoife made no sound and no movement.

"Has she spoken at all?" Jerome asked. It took Jeanne a minute to register that the young paramedic was staring directly at her and, in response, she shook her head. She grew more anxious and wearier by the second and the words that had bombarded Judy so freely earlier had dried up.

Toby on the other hand was becoming more and more fidgety now that he had thawed out a little. He wasn't sure what to make of all the commotion, so he barked and he barked, and when he wasn't getting the desired result, he barked some more.

Having watched Jeanne struggle to contain and silence the dog under her blanket, Bella made her way to the car and retrieved a scarf. She then returned to the barn and lowering herself to Toby's level, spoke to him very gently while stroking his ear; and then when she felt it appropriate, she fed the scarf through the loop in his collar. Momentarily, the dog was quiet, distracted by the attention. Once the scarf was securely threaded, she allowed him to jump off the bale while she attempted to coax him away from the scene.

Once on the barn floor, Toby simply tried to pull himself free, his bell ringing vigorously with his struggle. *He sounds like one of Father Christmas's reindeer*, Bella thought. When Toby's attempts to free himself became fruitless, he simply sat down anchoring his bottom firmly onto the barn floor. Pulling him simply resulted in Toby sliding across the floor on his bottom and Bella imagined splinters or straw being lodged in all the wrong places and thought better of this method. When Bella went to pick Toby up, he jumped back high on all fours and the bell jingled as Toby's head met Bella's chin. She cried out as she bit into her lip. For a moment, all eyes except Izzy's were on Bella while Toby remained relentless in his attempts to free himself from this constraint and return to where Aoife lay. With the fresh taste of blood in her mouth, Bella admitted defeat and remained exactly where she was, which was far enough away for the paramedics to attend to Aoife and close enough for Toby to have stopped barking as he simply watched the bodies milling around her. Jeanne moved towards Bella and handed her a pack of tissues in complete silence. She then returned to her previous spot and continued to watch as the paramedics took care of Aoife.

After recording Aoife's vital signs and having checked for injury, Izzy and Jerome lay the stretcher on bales of straw which Tom had been busy arranging at Izzy's request and both paramedics carefully lifted Aoife on to it.

At the sight of Aoife being carried out of the barn, Toby started jumping up to join her, his bell ringing urgently and his barks accompanying his plea. He then pulled hard on his makeshift lead, following as closely as able behind the paramedics.

Swiftly and adeptly, Jerome and Izzy lifted Aoife into the ambulance and onto the bed. Once Aoife was secured, Tom climbed in to the back, Izzy climbed in to the driver seat and Jerome shut the doors, on a whimpering dog. Izzy turned the ambulance around and passing the dog patrol van on the field, they drove back out up Mill Hill Farm Road in the direction of St Peters.

Toby was still whimpering when the police dog patrol car pulled up and lifted him in to the back. Toby's owner had been contacted and would collect him at the station.

14th December Aoife

Aoife was cold. Colder than she had ever felt before. Even colder than when Daddy and her had taken part in the 'ice bucket challenge'.

She could barely move her fingers and clinging on to the reindeer was difficult for her in the storm where the wind seemed to be trying hard to blow her off. She looked down. Gingerbread sat between her legs, nestling into her coat and she lowered her body to shelter a little more from the onslaught of the grumpy wind. She would have asked Gingerbread for his input but her lips and cheeks were so cold; it was like pins were pricking in to them.

Aoife wasn't quite sure how Gingerbread even managed to stay on but somehow the dog didn't move—not a whisker or a paw, a tail or an eyelid. Gingerbread simply remained fixed in the same position.

The reindeer whooshed at lightning speed through the wind and although Aoife was grateful for the lift, she was so tired trying to hold on and she wished he could slow down just a little. Her arms ached, her legs ached and her bottom was a little sore from the lack of padding beneath her cheeks.

Just as she had finished that thought, the snow, soft like cotton wool, was growing in size and translucent until the snowstorm turned in to thunderous hale and the wind blew angrier than before.

The hale pounded upon her like Tess's mean words so Aoife gripped her legs tighter around the stag, determined not to cry, and she fought the sensation to blow on her numb fingers to warm them up.

All at once, the deer shot up, avoiding a near collision with a tree top and all at once, Aoife was catapulted off his back, unable to maintain a grip and she began falling.

As her leg slid over his back, she clipped Gingerbread and he also lost his grip.

Aoife let out an inaudible scream and Gingerbread's legs splayed in all directions as he attempted to right his upside-down body. However, within moments, both lay upside-down on a white virgin ground surrounded by trees.

Gingerbread lay a short distance from Aoife and for a moment, they were both stunned—statuesque.

Aoife could still hear the jingle of her dashing guardian's bell and the desperate grunts the deer made but she couldn't see anything through the snow, above the trees. She went to shout in spite of the pain in her mouth, but the volume was turned down to just above mute as she tried to get her mouth to move. She didn't even know the deer's name.

"Hello!" she tried again, willing her voice to boom, "Help! I'm down here." she tried once more, but the words were carried along on the wind and her tears began to fall and she wished for sleep just for a moment.

Gingerbread had recovered his posture and gingerly made his way to Aoife's side. He licked the teardrops from her cheek and Aoife hugged him tight as they both shivered from the cold.

Aoife called out once more, "Over here! I'm here in the woods" her attempts a little more audible this time. She could hear the deer's grunts and the unmistakable jingle of his bell—sometimes loud and sometimes not—until eventually, the jingling was gone, and she and Gingerbread were all alone on the bed of white snow, until the only sound was the wind whistling through the trees and the periodic falling of clumps of snow from their branches.

With not much to see, no signs to give them a clue, Aoife felt very lost. She reached for her backpack, unable to feel it even though she could see the straps pressed tight against her coat.

Pulling off her gloves finger by finger with her teeth, her lips barely pursed, she pressed her hands up against her mouth and attempted to blow.

She blew for quite some time, her lips and fingers began to thaw, paining her as the cold left them. Once movement was restored, she reached for her backpack and there on top, she picked up Stick.

"Stick, until the North Star is visible and the moon shines the way, I don't know where to go to find home, can you help me?" she whispered, her lips paining with each syllable.

She held Stick out in front of her just like she had before and watched as Stick wobbled and then pointed her in the direction of the denser woods.

Aoife looked through the trees, into the shadows, and she could not see anything but a tiny glimmer of light from somewhere deep within. She found that light a little mesmerising, it reminded her of Grandad's fireplace and she was tempted, so tempted.

Aoife looked at Gingerbread, "What do you think?" she asked. Gingerbread barked and jumped around in circles over and over, his bell jingled and jangled in accompaniment. Aoife stared a little amused but unable to translate Gingerbread's movements in to words. "Shall we go this way?" she asked, looking in to the dark. Gingerbread barked again and stopped his twirling and instead jumped in and out of the snow; he encouraged Aoife to move forward.

Aoife was now in a dilemma as Stick had helped them before when Gingerbread hadn't been much help at all. If she was honest, and she always tried to be, she would rather follow Gingerbread than make her way into the dark woods.

Aoife apologised to Stick for not taking its advice before placing Stick back in her rucksack, not wanting to lose him in the woods.

Aoife's gloves were wet from the storm so she placed them in her pocket and pulled her coat sleeves down over her hand. Then tucking her hands under opposite armpits, she marched on behind Gingerbread, her legs aching and numb, and she hoped that they'd be home by dinnertime.

The thought of home made her miss her mummy and daddy and Aubrey and even Spark. She couldn't wait to tell them about her visit to Father Christmas and his wisdom about the Christmas Spirit.

Aoife wasn't sure how long she had been walking. The snow seemed to go on forever and there appeared to be no end in sight. She closed her eyes really tight and wished for Father Christmas and wondered if he would have sent a search party to find her when the deer returned and told him that he'd dropped her.

She'd watched a rescue on the TV once, ages ago when she was still five, about some people who got stuck on a big mountain and the other people came in a helicopter and took them to hospital. Aoife knew she didn't need to go to hospital, she was perfectly fine, just cold, just so very cold.

But she wished somebody would take her home on a helicopter before deciding she would in fact prefer to ride on a unicorn. She smiled at that thought and as she did, she felt her cheeks burn from the cold.

She's not sure why she hadn't noticed before, but Gingerbread's bell had stopped ringing even though Aoife could clearly see it bobbing up and down every time Gingerbread came bounding back as if to check Aoife was still behind him.

In fact, the wind had also stopped whistling. She couldn't hear the crunching of the snow and Gingerbread made no paw prints at all.

When she opened her mouth to say, "Gingerbread," it, too, was inaudible. She watched as a clump of snow fell and hit the ground yet still, there was not a single sound and a sensation which she had only felt after a nightmare before consumed her all at once and froze her to the spot.

The only thing she could hear was her thoughts, the sadness rose and she could no longer swallow it down. The screams raced around her head as the shadows closed in.

After a short while, she could hear a faint, distant voice. "Aoife…Aoife…oh, sweetheart, can you hear me?" Aoife looked around; she couldn't see anybody. She didn't recognise the voice but she decided it sounded kind. For a minute, the shadows stopped.

The voice seemed to come from above and all around. She opened her mouth to respond but nothing came out. "I'm here. Over here," she tried but the words rested only in her mind and her mouth wouldn't move to let them out.

"Aoife, you're going to be fine. Wake up. Come on, sweetheart, wake up!"

I am awake, Aoife thought. "I'm in the woods, over here," and she tried to wave her arms but they didn't move. "Hello, where are you?" she asked, none of her words escaping her mouth. They once again travelled around her head, refusing to make their way out.

The voice fell silent and the shadows moved in again. "Hello, help, I'm scared," but the words stayed locked in and no reply came back.

Gingerbread was still bounding up ahead and he turned around to see how far they'd walked and right behind her, she saw the imprint of their fall and she realised they'd been walking for a long time and getting nowhere at all.

"Hello," she tried once more. There was nothing, no voice to comfort her and Aoife sat down, unable to take the cold anymore. Just as she was ready to drift, the voice came back.

"Aoife…Aoife, tell me what you want for Christmas? I bet you will get some wonderful gifts, a good girl like you maybe even a whole sack. What do you think? I know you've been very good."

Aoife felt safe with the voice that was gentle and comforting and she thought for just a moment then asked, "Are you my Christmas Spirit?" but the words whirled around her head, her mouth still refused to move and the voice so soft and kind didn't respond. Aoife let the tiredness take her as Gingerbread lay down beside her.

She wanted to go home.

Just before the brain fell silent, before the shadows blocked her sight, before the nothingness stole her, she heard the kind, gentle voice sing a familiar Christmas song. Aoife began to hum along, the sound bouncing around in her mind, until the voice faded out and she succumbed.

14th December 15:40
Fred and Jeanne

Jeanne and Fred didn't tell Aubrey about Aoife. They weren't quite sure how to find the words to explain or indeed what to say so instead, they kept up the pretence and took him for a pizza and a play in the ball pen.

When Jen's call came in, Jeanne resorted to bribery promising Aubrey, "If we go now, we can all watch Puff the Magic Dragon at home a bit later." This time it was Fred's turn to raise an eyebrow.

Aubrey stopped throwing Spark down the slide and into the pit and stood up willingly, dressed willingly, and put on his shoes willingly while Fred paid the bill and had the barely touched pizza packed in to a doggy bag.

They then marched Aubrey to the car park while he held on to their hands, swinging between them, while Spark was tucked safely under Jeanne's arm and Fred carried the pizza.

Fred let Aubrey press the button to open the doors of his grandad's car and strapped him in to his chair. Aubrey fell asleep before they'd reached the car park exit.

14th December 15:55
Jeanne Taylor and Judy

Jeanne sat in her living room with her foil blanket still wrapped around her shoulders, a cup of tea in front of her and a plate of bourbon biscuits which Judy had found in a tin in the cupboard.

Jeanne hadn't said much since the ambulance left and she barely seemed to be present on the walk back up Mill Hill Farm Road, so Judy decided to stay with her while waiting for her friend to arrive.

"Will you…will somebody let me know how Aoife is doing?" Jeanne asked Judy. "I would really like to know that she's…well, that she's okay. She is so small." Jeanne stared in to the distance for a minute. "What on earth…?" She sipped on her tea and didn't complete the question which was on everyone's lips.

Judy said, "I'm sure somebody will be in touch," which was in fact the truth as the police would need a statement from her, but it wasn't protocol for them to share information other than with immediate family.

The doorbell rang. Judy got up from her armchair and answered. She briefly filled Carlos in on Jeanne's ordeal before announcing, "Jeanne, it's Carlos."

A stocky man with a balding head stood in the doorway, Jeanne looked up and at the sight of her friend, she let go and the flood gates opened, releasing an afternoon's tension.

As Carlos embraced his friend, Judy said, "Bye," and left. Outside, she paused, inhaling deeply as if her lungs had been starved of oxygen and releasing again, she stepped forward down the steps onto the pavement and headed towards her car.

14th December 16:00
Fred and Jeanne

"Shouldn't we just get to the hospital?" Fred asked.

"We need to get some clothes for Aoife," Jeanne responded with that tone that said, 'don't challenge me on this'.

"But…" logic told Fred that surely, they would be better off seeing their granddaughter, seeing Jen, Perry, and the doctors, and then deciding what was needed. He saw little gain in having to do a job twice, especially as he would be doing the driving. He immediately chastised himself for fussing over trivia.

As they drove down Burgundy Road towards number 34, they were both relieved to see that the press had dispersed. A single photographer stood beside an old Escort and snapped away as Jeanne got out of the car. Jeanne paid him no attention and kept her head down. Fred remained in the driving seat with a sleeping Aubrey in the back.

Harjot was descending the steps and Fred watched as Jeanne and he spoke for a moment and the house key was exchanged. Jeanne then entered their daughter's home and Harjot disappeared towards the parked police car down the road.

A few more snaps from the photographer before he, too, climbed in to the Escort and drove away.

Jeanne emerged ten minutes later with a suitcase, big enough for a week's stay, for a large family.

Fred grabbed the case just as Jeanne reached the bottom step and once it was in the boot of the car and Jeanne was strapped in, Fred checked for the best route to St Peters. At

16:13, it was the onset of rush-hour traffic and Sat Nav directed them down Cherry Lane. They would arrive at St Peters within 30 minutes according to the male anatomic voice of the inbuilt navigation.

Aubrey remained in his slumber with Spark tucked under his arm.

Jeanne mentally walked through what she had packed for Aoife: reindeer pyjamas, dressing gown, hairbands, Aoife's favourite brush that didn't hurt when it detangled her locks, toothbrush, shower gel, her favourite cotton joggers and a soft woollen jumper that didn't scratch.

Just in case, she added several pairs of knickers and vests, and then another jumper and joggers.

In the cupboard next to the tea caddy, she found a packet of rich tea biscuits, Aoife's favourite since a toddler. She snatched a couple of bananas from the fruit bowl on the breakfast bar for Jen and Perry, noticing that the kitchen was clean of dishes with the exception of the cups that had multiplied in the sink since they had left to collect Aubrey from nursery.

They must be hungry, she thought, and then for good measure, she added a packet of breadsticks, chocolate digestives and some apples. From the kettle she had boiled on her way in, she made up a flask of coffee on her way out.

She noticed Fred's expression at the size of the case as she pulled it down the stairs but she wanted to be prepared, didn't want to worry, didn't want Jen and Perry to be bothered unduly about anything other than their daughter, her granddaughter. She hated this feeling in her stomach; a feeling of almighty fear of not being in control, of not being able to fix it and of feeling superfluous all at once.

So, Jeanne had to do something, even if it was pre-empting how this nightmare day would play out: grabbing clothes and food, and visualising them all crying with relief at Aoife's bedside while she ate too many rich tea biscuits and Jen looked on with mock disapproval was about all she felt qualified to do at this time.

Jeanne's phone pinged at 16:20, it was a text from Jen. They were at the hospital. All the information Jen sent was the ward and room name and instructions on where best to park.

Jeanne waited for a moment hoping to hear how Aoife is.

"Jen says park in the small car park near A&E, the one close to outpatients," Jeanne said, looking at Fred. Fred nodded, giving Jeanne a momentary glance but said nothing.

Jeanne simply responded to Jen, "Okay, seen you in twit minus," which ought to have been, "Okay, see you in twenty minutes." Jeanne despaired of predictive text and her continuous failure to check before pressing send.

"It's odd, don't you think?" Fred said.

It had struck him from the minute he entered Jen and Perry's house earlier that day that something was missing, as if joy wasn't there, as if joy had left before his granddaughter. It had taken him a moment to realise that the thing which was absent was Christmas.

His daughter, Jen, had always loved Christmas, "Can we get the tree this weekend?" she'd ask when not much older than Aoife.

"No, it's still only November," he'd say.

A tradition she kept up with a wink and a smile into her teens. "We'll get it on the first weekend in December like we always do," and inevitably, a disappointed Jen would skulk away feeling a big injustice was being done and try again another day, unable to wait a moment longer for Christmas to descend on their cottage.

This tradition of a Christmas tree on the first weekend had continued when Jen moved out. He and Jen would have an unspoken date to pick one out and when Jen and Perry met and married, the tradition continued between the couple.

"What's odd?" Jeanne asked.

"Ummm…oh…I was just wondering why there were no Christmas decorations in their house. Jen and Perry love Christmas and, well, Aoife…she loves that tree," he responded.

"Yes, I suppose," Jeanne responded and wondered how it hadn't occurred to her. Fred was right, there was no sign of

Christmas in 34 Burgundy Road at all, not even the smells of spiced potpourri or Jen's cinnamon candles.

Conversation and contemplation ceased when Fred turned left into St Peters and concentrated on which direction he needed to drive and where he could park.

His heart was pounding in anticipation of the news. He felt it might burst from his chest so he took several deep breaths and headed straight across the roundabout towards Accident & Emergency.

Jeanne's heart was racing. She closed her eyes. *Be strong,* she thought, recognising this as one of the biggest roles of her life. *Park that control in the bay,* she thought to herself, not really knowing where that phraseology sprung from but she knew what she meant.

Fred drove through the barrier grabbing the last parking space and Jeanne made her way to the boot, grabbed the buggy and unstrapped Aubrey from his booster seat as carefully as she could, then strapped him in to his buggy while Fred grabbed the case and lowered the boot with a less than delicate slam.

With one eye open, Aubrey looked at Fred, "Aubrey do it!" he said and wriggled himself to a more comfortable position. Fred smiled at him and handed him the keys. Aubrey pressed the button, watching the lights flash and listening to the two beeps in quick succession as the doors locked. He smiled up at his grandad.

"Hi, love, were her. Mx," Jeanne wrote and pressed send. She then pushed the buggy through the doors of the A&E department, not offering any explanation to Aubrey who was soaking up the surroundings.

Jeanne's phone pinged, *"Go to the family room, will see you in there. Jx."*

Even though Jeanne was fully aware of the emergency, fully aware of the pressure and pain her daughter was under, she still felt a momentary pang of hurt from Jen's vague responses. As soon as the emotion reared itself, she banished her own feelings of inadequacy.

With that in mind, she approached the reception area to enquire where they needed to go. "Yes, Aoife…Aoife Mercier. She was brought in within the last hour or so."

The receptionist checked the system. "Yes, she's in the Intensive Care," the man at the desk responded and proceeded to give directions.

Jeanne stopped him and said, "We were asked to wait in the family room."

"Yes, it's close by, you'll see a sign post for it once you hit the ward," the man advised.

"Thank you," Jeanne responded and made way for the next person in the queue.

Fred, having listened in on the discussion, took the lead, knowing his wife couldn't find her way out of a paper bag. How many texts had he had at work simply stating, "I'm last," which he knew by now meant, 'I'm lost,' expecting him to navigate her out of a park, or a town and even a walk in the woods that he'd never been on.

For all of her control, strength, organisation and intelligence, what Fred loved most about Jeanne were her faux pars; how she couldn't send a text that made sense, how she would swear they needed to go right when the directions clearly stated left, how she never remembered a film she watched, how she consistently forgot the name of actors, and how she mixed up metaphors when trying to convey a serious point and how she turned from rigid to silly after a few glasses of wine.

He loved every bone in her body even when, or perhaps especially when, she was a little cross with him. He had understood a long time ago: if she didn't care, then she would have no emotion toward him either way, so he was happy to take what she gave and in truth, he found winding her up amusing—a sport.

It is no problem at all to get her to go from 0 to 60 on the frustration scale. And he loved how when she'd realised his game, she would chastise him and would stomp off like a four-year-old.

Aubrey had been very quiet up until now. However, on hearing his sister's name, he said, "Fifi coming?"

"Soon, darling," Jeanne responded, pushing his buggy towards the ward.

"Fifi got a sprise?" Aubrey asked.

Jeanne, not quite understanding, said, "I'm not sure," and continued pushing the buggy down the long corridor.

Fred slowed down for Jeanne to catch up as they approached the ward. Its blue door was adorned with a picture of a unicorn in a rainbow forest. Fred's heart missed a beat and he choked, *Aoife would love this,* he thought, wishing Aoife never had to see it, never had to be here, wishing she was home asking him questions that he couldn't answer.

On his last visit, he had sat on the big red sofa, a book or three spread open in front of Aoife whose legs were crossed and her eyes piercing as she began her interrogation of her grandad. All that was missing for him was a spotlight and the Mastermind theme tune. She, at six years old, was every bit as intimidating as Magnus Magnusson, he felt.

"What's the number before infinity?" she asked.

"Let's google it," he said.

"That's funny, Grandad, it's Googol."

"I know, that's what I said, let's Google it."

Aoife had laughed the kind of laugh that was contagious like an itch to be scratched, her whole body shaking, tears rolling down her cheeks uncontrollably and he in stitches although he didn't quite get the joke.

She then nestled in to him, her small arms wrapped around his neck before kissing him on the cheek and explaining as if he were the child and she the wise oracle. *She was,* he thought. *She is,* he corrected. He wouldn't imagine life without her light in it.

After a moment where nothing but a breath filled the space, Aoife asked, "Grandad, did you know that Beluga whales love music?"

He had merely responded with "Ummm", placing his finger on his lips and looking up as if the ceiling were about to remind him but nothing dropped in.

Aoife broke the silence and continued, "Grandad, did you know that Scrooge didn't celebrate Christmas with the Cratchits?"

He did know that and, for a moment, he had actually felt pleased with himself.

Fred was snapped back to the present when Jeanne pressed the buzzer. Some words were exchanged between Jeanne and the person on the intercom and once inside, they asked for the family room and the nurse who was flicking through notes didn't look up but simply said, "Second door on the right."

14th December 16:45
Fred, Jeanne and Aubrey

Aubrey was playing with the colourful beads on the roller-coaster table in the corner of the family room. He'd been plied with cold pizza and ice-cold water from the water fountain, and Fred had read him a page from Puff the Magic Dragon which he'd found on a bookshelf near the entrance. But so far, there was no sign of Jen and Perry.

Fred watched his wife, her complexion grey, her eyes darting each time the door opened or shut. If she had her way, he knew she'd be in the ward demanding news but she didn't, and he knew how difficult that restraint would be for her.

Fred diverted his focus to Aubrey who still didn't understand why he was there and where Mummy and Daddy were, but for the most part, he was content with the books or the toys. And *Thank heaven for Spark,* he thought. This focus stopped Fred thinking about the reason for them being there. In truth, he wanted to stop thinking full-stop for a minute.

Jeanne watched as Fred busied himself with Aubrey: a story, a toy, the hopping of Spark across the chairs and floor as he made dinosaur sounds with Aubrey laughing so much that it boomed around the room as if there were no care in the world.

How does he manage to…she searched for the words, be normal, she thought, doesn't he care? She banished the words so unkind and unfair. Don't deflect your frustration, Jeanne McKinlay, she chastised. A plethora of thoughts circulated her mind as she wondered what the wait could mean, and every time she dared to believe no news is good news, she still prepared herself for the worst all of the time, reining her emotions back in as the worst was unspeakable.

14th December 16:45
Jen and Perry

On arrival, Aoife's wet clothes had been stripped and she was wrapped in blue cotton blankets and sheets. There she lay swallowed up in the adult-size hospital bed. A cannula fed in to her arm and a mask of humidified oxygen was placed over her airways to warm her up, but Aoife remained in the same state of hypothermia as when the ambulance wheeled her in— as when she was found in the barn.

This was the sight that Jen and Perry were met with when Tom opened the door after preparing them.

Jen shed no tears, she daren't break, she simply wished Aoife would cry, make a fuss, move a finger, anything but this. Aoife's eyes remained firmly shut, barely a twitch of life.

Jen held her hand as she watched the saline from the cannula drip into Aoife's arm; she waited and willed her awake. Hadn't she written such a story: a child in hospital, a family distraught? All she thought then was whether her plot sounded believable; had she set the scene and would she, a parent, really behave like that if her child lay helpless, unresponsive, hurt? She wrote of how the mother and father cried at the bedside and yet here she was, here they were, staring at their child, not a teardrop between them.

Be strong, she told herself, Aoife mustn't hear the whimpers. *Open the flood gates,* she told herself, *and you may not stop,* and as for the, 'Why? Why did her daughter leave the house?' There were no answers to that, no clues on her person.

Perry and Jen had barely spoken a word since the doctor left. So many questions aired and so many 'We don't know at this stage' answers.

"She has lay wet from the rain and slept in the freezing cold for up to eight hours or more that we know of. The important thing is to restore her temperature so that it normalises and stabilises at 37 degrees Celsius. Currently, it's below 35 degrees Celsius. We will know more over the next couple of hours and will reassess at that time," the doctor had spoken slowly and purposefully, as if they themselves were children and they had felt such as they digested every word, weighing up the gravity of the situation.

And so, Jen and Perry sat in their impatience, watching the seconds and minutes, waiting for change as the nurses periodically checked the vitals on the machine, noting observations on the chart which hung at the bottom of the bed.

"We should go and see Mum, Dad and Aubrey," Jen said, looking at Perry. "What will we tell Aubrey?" she asked, but Perry looked at her with nothing to offer.

As they stood, he said, "The truth, we have to tell him the truth."

Jen nodded, not entirely sure what that was, but realised she had jumped ahead in her thought process and she decided telling him what they know now was the best place to start and finish.

In the corridor of the ward, Jen and Perry approached the nurse's desk and explained they would be in the family room for a moment with relatives.

The nurse nodded, giving them a knowing smile, full of sympathy and Perry wanted to shout, 'Wipe the pity off your face!' But he didn't, he simply followed Jen, passing rooms with other children and other parents. *Were they equally so desperate?* Perry thought, and then he stopped, unable to carry the weight of that possibility and probability on the ward.

14th December 17:10
The Family Room

"Should I go and check?" Jeanne was saying just as the door opened up and Jen and Perry walked in.

"Mummy! Daddy!" Aubrey screamed, not knowing which one to run to at first, so he aimed for both, wrapping one arm around his mummy's leg and the other around his daddy's as he held on tight.

"Hello, munchkin," they both said, almost in unison, as Aubrey held up his arms and Perry swooped him up.

Lifting his hands, Aubrey placed both on his daddy's cheeks before rapidly withdrawing them as he said, "Daddy's scratchy."

Perry rubbed his hand across his face, the stubble was a little prickly and he smiled at Aubrey, saying, "Sorry."

Aubrey stared at him, not shifting his gaze at all. Perry pulled a face and opened his eyes wide then stuck out his tongue and Aubrey laughed as Perry moved to a chair and sat them both down.

Jen stood in the warm embrace of her mother. She inhaled the scent of aloe vera and lavender and, just for a moment, felt like a five-year-old again—feeling that familiar urge to abandon herself to her mother's will. But she wasn't a child, and so she didn't.

Fred observed and Jeanne glanced at him over Jen's shoulder. Eventually, Jeanne released her embrace and pushed Jen gently from her and said, "Come on, sit down."

Aubrey sat on Perry's knee watching. He jumped down grabbing Spark from Grandad, and, jumping on his knee, he asked, "Where's Fifi?" aiming the question at Mummy.

Seconds stretched before Jen or Perry spoke. In the end, it was Perry who said, "Aoife's a little bit poorly."

"Fifi need medicine?" Aubrey interjected.

"Yes," Jen responded. "Aoife is in bed and she is being given medicine in her arm and she has to wear a mask."

Aubrey thought for a minute and said, "Fifi got a Spider-man mask?" None of the adults could help their smile.

"No," Perry said. " It's an oxygen mask, Aubrey." And pre-empting Aubrey's next question, he said, "It's to help Aoife get warm because she got very cold when she went for a walk."

Jeanne and Fred were listening attentively. When Aubrey stopped speaking, it was Fred who asked, "What's wrong with Aoife?"

"Hypothermia," Jen responded. "The police believe Aoife fell asleep in the barn in the early hours, wet and frozen. There was rain and sleet overnight and again throughout the day…" Jeanne and Fred nodded, agreeing with that statement, "and where she lay, there were gaps in the roof and the walls so the sub-zero temperature and the strong winds…" Jen stopped, as if not knowing or wishing to complete the sentence.

Perry leaned forward and grabbed her hand. She looked at him, fighting the urge to break, and he squeezed her hands between his before continuing, "Due to the sub-zero tempera-tures, her body was unable to maintain its core temperature and now, at this moment, her temperature is below 35 degree Celsius." He paused, trying to recall all that they knew up to now. "Tom, the inspector, also suggested if it wasn't for Toby, the dog that was with Aoife, well…" the pause hung in the air as Perry focused on his hands around his wife's, "Toby had his head across her and…" he didn't finish.

"We're waiting for the doctors to make a decision on what next," Perry concluded, breaking the silence.

"Can we see her?" Jeanne asked.

"Yes," Jen said, and then looking at Aubrey, she said, "Remember, Aoife has some medicine going in to her arm and a mask, so she won't be able to speak to you right now, munchkin, okay?"

Aubrey nodded and then slid off his grandad's knee and headed for the door.

Jeanne picked up the bag containing the remnant of pizza, her own handbag and stood up. She then walked towards the suitcase which sat in the corner of the room close to the bookshelf. Jen looked at her dad and Fred lifted his shoulders and winked at her in that knowing way, and Jen decided to leave it there.

As Jeanne turned, rolling the case towards her kin, she said, "I've brought Aoife's favourite pyjamas and some rich tea. She'll be hungry when she wakes."

"Thank you, Jeanne," Perry responded. Jen pushed the door open and led the way to Aoife's room.

14th December 17:30
The Decision

Jen reached the door first with Perry trailing behind, holding Aubrey's hand, and Fred pulling the case while Jeanne pushed the folded-up buggy.

As she looked through the glass, Jen saw nurses and doctors busying themselves around Aoife's bed.

"Mum, Dad, could you go and get some coffees please?" Jen said, looking at Aubrey then to the door and then back at them again, more urgency in her voice than she planned. *No fuss now, Mum, no questions,* she thought.

Jeanne and Fred nodded and looking at Aubrey, Jeanne said, "Who wants to go and get some sweets?"

Even then, Jen couldn't help herself giving her mother a look that said, 'Really!'

Jeanne could feel the stare but ignored her daughter and those magic words didn't entice Aubrey. It didn't even raise interest in him. So, Jeanne bent over in front of him, "Can you come and help me find the coffee and chocolate please, Aubrey?" Jeanne tried again.

Aubrey looked past Jeanne to his parents, his head turning from one to the other, his feet firmly planted and his lip beginning to quiver as he pressed Spark under his chin, squashing the dinosaur against his chest with his folded arms; he wept.

"I'll go," Perry said in spite of the fact that he wanted to go nowhere, but he knew looking at Aubrey's face what would ensue if they forced his hand. Perry looked at Fred and Fred wheeled the case behind his grandson and son-in-law down the corridor, away from the Intensive Care and through the unicorn double doors to the lift, while Jeanne went and stood beside her daughter, glimpsing the commotion behind the door.

Jen looked at her mother, placed her hand upon the handle of the door and pushed.

Jeanne closed the door behind her, Jen stood watching her finger quickly finding her lips and her body began swaying, rocking anxiety in check. The words that she planned on spouting, "Is she okay?" stuck, pursed between her lips. *Does this look like okay?* she reprimanded her thoughts before the first word escaped.

Jeanne glimpsed the small unicorn bag over the nurse's shoulder in the corner of the room, but she couldn't see her granddaughter with the bustle of blue uniforms around her bed.

Nobody had noticed them enter but very quickly the doctor, Doctor Baav, who Jen had met earlier, emerged from within the circle and spotted her.

"Mrs Mercier, Jen…Aoife's organ function is being compromised, I'd like to try irrigation to warm them up. We need to act now." Jen looked on and then around the room, staring straight through her mother in search of Perry, feeling so small and unable to make such a decision on her own before realising she had no idea what decision she was being asked to make at all.

"I don't understand," she said. "What is irrigation?" she asked.

Doctor Baav explained, "Irrigation means we take a warm saltwater solution and apply it by catheter to the organs, in this case the lungs and abdominal area, with the aim of warming them up so that her temperature will rise. Without intervention, her organs will fail." Jen couldn't help but notice the emphasis on 'will'. There was a pause as the doctor looked at Aoife, "Jen, we haven't seen enough improvement…and her organs," Doctor Baav didn't say anymore. She placed a hand on Jen's and reiterated, "We need to act now."

With tears running down her cheek onto her finger and down her hand, Jen snapped back to the 'now' and looked at

Doctor Baav as if seeing her for the first time and she nodded. Then she nodded again before whispering, "Okay."

Jeanne had already left the room and outside, she dialled Perry's number, it went straight to voice. She dialled again and again, and she texted but it wouldn't send, and she rang again.

"Where's the cafeteria please?" she asked a nurse rushing past. The nurse didn't stop as she raced into an adjacent room. Jeanne heard the alarms as two more nurses rushed down the corridor.

Racing to the lift, Jeanne tried again. "Hello," came the reply.

All of her rehearsed calm had diluted with every attempt to reach her son-in-law until her words escaped directly—blunt. "Perry, thank God. You need to come upstairs now."

"What's happened?" Perry warbled.

"Just come…please. It's…well, the doctor. It's Aoife's…" the phone went dead.

Perry ran the three flights of stairs and burst through the door where he found Jen fixed to the spot.

Jen hadn't moved at all from when she had stepped in. She observed as if floating above, watching everyone rush and fuss around Aoife as Aoife lay unmoving, unprotesting in the midst of the swarming of blue uniforms around her bed.

Jen could neither move toward her nor could she seem to move away and so she stared, eyes transfixed as her daughter was attended to, as if they both were in a slowed-down version of the same scene.

Jeanne looked out of the glass window, there was no sign of Fred or Aubrey, so she headed out with a nod to Perry and took the lift to reception.

Wiping her tears, Jeanne stood up straight, brushed her clothes into presentable and her hair from her face as she brushed it with her fingernails. She then took a deep breath and walked towards Fred and Aubrey. Aubrey was trying to escape his booster seat in the cafeteria close to the hospital exit. "Hey, what's all this fuss?" she said in her softest grandma voice.

Five minutes later, they led a screaming Aubrey who was digging his heels into the solid underfoot and pulling in the direction of where they had left his bottom first as he shouted, "NO!" over and again at the top of his voice.

Jeanne couldn't help but blush at being the centre of stares and glares but nobody said a word, not the passers-by, patients or nurses. In the car, they eventually managed to strap in his rigid body as he sat sobbing for his mummy and daddy. Even Spark offered little comfort to him now.

By the time Fred pulled up at 34 Burgundy Road, Aubrey had fallen asleep. No words had been uttered between Jeanne and Fred.

Fred was still in the dark as to what was going on with his granddaughter.

14th December 19:00
Fred, Jeanne and Aubrey

Once bathed, with his eyes still red from sobbing, Aubrey sat down with Jeanne to watch 'In the Night Garden'. Dressed in his dinosaur pyjamas, he snuggled in close to his grandma and they remained that way for a while.

There had been no word from Jen and Perry other than to acknowledge Jeanne's text to let them know of their whereabouts.

Fred arrived back from collecting some clothes and essentials from their house, then sat with his wife and grandson until the episode had finished by which time Aubrey had given in to exhaustion.

Fred lifted his grandson into his bed, pulled his duvet under his chin and placed Spark next to him. He stood in the doorway, watching him sleep for a minute, before sitting down with his wife and placing her hand in his. Jeanne looked at her husband with fondness and sadness intermingled and began to explain all that she knew from the five minutes in the room.

Fred listened, not interrupting her and when she had finished, he pulled her close and they held one another, consumed by their own thoughts.

Jeanne got up to make tea. There was no word from the hospital so she picked up her phone and texted Jen, *"I love you,"* and pressed send.

Fred was flicking channels, unable to find anything to watch, anything to drag him from his all-consuming thoughts. He then switched the TV off.

Jeanne sat on the corner of the sofa, her legs curled up, sipping her night-time tea and staring at nothing in particular.

Fred was looking around his daughter's home, feeling even more saddened at the lack of festivity displays within when they heard Aubrey's door open. Jeanne placed her cup on the table and stood up walking towards the sound. Fred watched on.

Aubrey emerged from his bedroom clutching Spark and didn't appear to see or notice Jeanne at all as he made his way to Aoife's room. Once there, he opened the door and walked towards the bed.

Jeanne quickly followed not uttering a word and watched as Aubrey climbed onto Aoife's bed and lay down. She carefully tucked him under the duvet and ensured Spark was right beside him.

"He was sleepwalking," Jeanne said, looking at Fred when she returned. "I might finish my tea and go myself. You okay on the sofa?" she asked, knowing that there was no alternative. They weren't sure if Perry or Jen would come home.

"I'll be fine," Fred responded as Jeanne put the dishes in the bowl in the sink. She then bent over and kissed her husband before grabbing her phone to check for messages. There were none, and laying it down on Aoife's bedside table, she slipped in to Aoife's bed next to Aubrey, who lay star-shaped with Spark over his eye.

14th December 18:30
Jen and Perry

Jen can barely remember the walk to the family room as the nurses ushered them away from Aoife while the medical staff set about fitting the catheter.

It wasn't long before a doctor, not Doctor Baav, was telling them how that had gone well and they could sit with Aoife now.

"No, there has been no change but it will take time," the doctor affirmed.

So, Perry and Jen assumed the same position, holding each of their daughter's hand from opposite sides of the bed and, for a minute, both just watched the machine as it monitored the heartbeat; they listened to the beep until the sound faded into background noise as they spoke to their daughter. "Aoife, when you come home…" Jen swallowed and bit her lip. "When…" the word broken…

"When you come home," Perry continued, "we'll take you to the cafe, you know, the one that sells tea and scones, oh, and don't tell your mummy but you can even have double cream."

Jen looked at Perry, chuckling between her tears. She grabbed a tissue from her trouser pocket and wiped them away.

"You'd better not," Jen replied looking at her daughter, waiting for her to giggle with the excitement of her and Daddy doing something a little naughty that Mummy wouldn't like.

But there was nothing. Aoife's eyes remained shut, her body remained still and Jen and Perry looked at one another and continued.

"Pumpkin, what would you like for Christmas?" As Jen asked, she realised she hadn't even seen Aoife's Christmas list, the one she would normally start in the summer. A pang of guilt rose. *I've been a terrible mother,* she thought.

"Didn't you say you would like the Lego Hogwarts Express?" Perry asked. Jen looked at Perry. How on earth could he know that when he was never home?

And just for a moment, a flicker in time, the old feelings of resentment rose. Quickly, she reminded herself they had no place here and had consumed so much energy already; and so, she let them go, felt them leave her.

"Wow, I wonder what Father Christmas will say to that. You'd better get that list sent off, Aoife, so he can make enough," she urged.

Aoife didn't join in: her eyes didn't open, her mouth didn't form a smile, she didn't jump about with excitement searching for an envelope or stamp and she didn't ask if the picture she had drawn would be liked by Father Christmas. She didn't do anything at all.

Perry stood up. "I'll get us coffee," he said, looking at Jen. "I won't be long, pumpkin, if you wake up, your mummy can text me and I'll grab you a drink, maybe even a rich tea biscuit," he said, looking at Aoife who slept motionless.

Once in the corridor, Perry struggled to compose himself. He leant up against the wall and then, bending over, he inhaled as if his lungs were depleted of oxygen.

"Can I get you anything?" the nurse in a green uniform asked.

Perry shook his head. "Thank you," he said and made his way to the exit in search of a coffee machine.

If he was honest, he simply needed to remove himself from the stifling confinement of the room in which his daughter, normally so full of life and so wise, was frightening him beyond any fear he had ever felt before.

And the knots, the churning within, wasn't subsiding and so he needed to breathe to stop the nausea overpowering him.

He stood outside and texted Fred, *"Aoife is stable. See you tomorrow."* Unsure what stable really means, he pressed send.

A message came back almost immediately, *"Okay. J and A asleep. Fred,"* and that's about all Perry needed to hear right now.

Jen leaned forward, pulling her chair almost in line with Aoife's face, she leant over and began to sing their song, the one which they had danced around the kitchen to, the one they had been singing since Aoife was two, the one that made the day brighter made the soul lighter, the one that made all worries fade, but Aoife didn't join in the chorus and Jen forgot the words so she hummed, and the hum faded away like the conversation previously.

"I love you, Aoife Mercier, it's time for you to wake up now." Jen kissed Aoife on her forehead and hoped that the desperation consuming her wasn't transferred by words to the depths where Aoife would hear.

The door flew open as Perry walked in with two coffees and two packets of crisps. "It's all I could find," he said.

"Thank you," Jen said, standing up to take a coffee and a packet for herself.

"No change," she said before the question passed his lips.

15th December 02:00
Jeanne and Fred

Jeanne sat upright with a start. In the first nano seconds of her awareness, she reminded herself where she was and then, she tried to find the source of the invasive music to mute it so that Aubrey didn't wake.

She traced it to the windowsill and there the alarm clock was flashing in multi-coloured lights; it was 2 a.m. Lifting her hand up, she pressed down on the top several times, shifting her hand across it, not quite sure how to switch it off. Eventually, she hit the right button.

Jeanne sat for a moment, her legs hanging over the bed, her elbows resting upon her legs, her head in her hands, before rubbing her eyes and standing up and heading out of the door towards the living room.

Fred had fallen asleep with the TV on and somebody or other was trying to sell jewellery as numbers flashed up on the screen with the promise of discount and two for one if you purchase them now. Jeanne found the remote secured under Fred's belly and switched it off.

Fred stirred and Jeanne sat on the coffee table, gently stroking his head and whispering, "Fred. Fred, wake up." Fred snored and grunted through his throat before murmuring a sleepy response that in fact translated in to no language at all. Jeanne watched, waiting, and as Fred fell back into his slumber, she brushed his hair again, "Fred, wake up. Wake up."

Fred broke wind and smiled but he didn't open his eyes. Jeanne stopped stroking his hair and shook him a little, her nose wrinkled from the smell and an involuntary "Uh," escaped her mouth. "Fred, it's about Aoife, wake up." This time, her tone firmer than before.

Fred opened one eye and screamed out.

"Shhhh, you'll wake Aubrey," Jeanne said sternly.

"What's the matter? Has something happened to…"

Jeanne didn't let him finish. "No, nothing's happened, but I know when Aoife left the house." She stopped for a minute, thinking about her statement. In truth, she knew when Aoife was awakened, not when she left.

Fred sat upright. "What do you mean?" he asked, he's now awake and waiting.

"Aoife's alarm clock went off at 2 a.m."

Fred, still staring at Jeanne, waited for the punchline. "Well, don't you see? We know Aoife was in the house until at least 2 a.m.," she said, waiting for him to catch up.

"Well, let's not jump to any conclusions," Fred said, "Maybe it's been like that for ages, maybe…"

"Why would Aoife need an alarm at 2 a.m.?" Jeanne asked. In truth, she would be happy for a plausible explanation right now, but Fred merely shrugged his shoulders and was out of reasons before he could think of any.

"So, we think Aoife left soon after 2 a.m. but where was she going?" he asked, wondering if Jeanne had any ideas on that too.

Jeanne shrugged. "I don't know," she responded. It seemed they had the 'when' but not the 'why'.

They both sat, their knees almost touching and their eyes locked as if seeing into each other's souls.

"Tea?" Fred asked.

Jeanne nodded then stood up at the same time as Fred and headed towards Aoife's bedroom to pick up her phone.

Aubrey lay fast asleep and she closed the door behind her as she pressed the button which lit up her phone; there were no new messages.

15th December 06:00
Jen and Perry

Jen woke in the armchair of the hospital room looking around to get her bearings. She wiped the sleep from her eyes and stretched her legs; they were aching from the position she had sat in. She couldn't say how long she'd slept as she had woken frequently with the nurses checking on Aoife.

She looked over at Perry slumped over the foot of Aoife's bed, his bottom resting on a grey, hard plastic chair and Aoife hadn't moved at all.

Outside of their room, Jen could hear the rattling of trays, and through the glass window, she imagined a shift change taking place as the nurses stood at the desk, charts in their hands and discussions ensuing between them as she stretched and watched, as if inside a goldfish bowl looking out.

She turned and stood beside Aoife, leaning over to kiss her forehead before taking her place beside the bed and lifting Aoife's fingers into her palm as she sat. "Good morning, pumpkin. It's time to wake up. I hope you've slept well."

Perry lifted his head. "Morning," he said.

"Morning," Jen responded without looking around.

"Coffee?" he asked.

Jen nodded. "Thank you."

Perry stretched, feeling the pain in his back from the position he had lay in. As Perry made his way to the door, Jen asked, "Can you get me a book please?"

"Which one?" Perry asked, before reminding himself they weren't at home.

He didn't wait for a response and Jen didn't give one. He smiled at the nurses busying themselves as he made his way to the family room. He's not even sure they saw him.

In the family room, he scanned the shelves and pulled out 'A Christmas Carol' and he dropped it off with Jen before heading for the gents and then the cafeteria for a coffee and, hopefully, something to eat although he wasn't sure he had an appetite.

When Perry opened the door, he noticed that the book which he had handed Jen a short while earlier lay open upon her lap. However, the story she recited was not the work of Mr Charles Dickens it was an original, and theirs. He listened attentively, aware all at once. His wife's gaze never left the face of their little girl. Jen's words spilled from her lips spouting sorrow and regret and hope of their child's forgiveness while searching for understanding all at once, to the why that had made her leave home. And weaving between the narrative was a display of love so deep so uncompromising for this child they had birthed. He listened as Jen continued.

"…100. Coming ready or not!

The little girl searched and searched, but her mummy and daddy could not be found.

Mummy was there in the house yet the girl could not reach her, as mummy sat trapped in her room guarded by words of warning weighted with threat and deadlines looming; note pads, pens, timetables beneath her spanning the breadth of the desk she leaned on. Books on shelves, too many to read: bound narrative of the lives of others and tales of make believe.

Mummy was removed from the real life story happening in the walls of their home. This, their life story, was stuck in the planning phase as she built tomorrows dreams and future nest eggs, as she scribed fictitious text.

The parents laid foundations. Today turned into tomorrow's play and tomorrow never came. And patiently the girl waited. And then the girl wondered.

Was she invisible; was she not really there at all?

The daddy was busy crunching numbers and sitting on aeroplanes, and he definitely could not be seen for days, sometimes even weeks—he was excellent at the game of hide-and-seek.

Sat in a different country he presented those numbers at meetings, in power-points, promising to improve upon the improved."

Perry wanted to protest, jump in with justification, but he didn't; he couldn't.

"Perhaps the little girl had made her parents up? Jen continued.

"This game of hide-and-seek is quite a feat, it isn't like hiding in the wardrobe, the door ajar, or behind the curtain feet sticking out or like making yourself small behind the sofa, your head betraying your hiding spot. The girl could see the grownups very well, but they didn't see what was in front of them.

Come out, come out wherever you are." Jen whispered.

"110, 111, 112…" Aoife's eyes remained closed.

"The parents emerged from their hiding place to find their little girls eyes firmly shut, hiding in plain sight.

"Open your eyes pumpkin," her mummy said. We can see now. Open your eyes please, we're sorry it's taken so long. The count is over we're here, come home.

You are our sun, moon and North Star. Tell us, what spell will wake you up?

A kiss from mummy and another from daddy? You can have a thousand and a thousand more; a million gazillion and the same again. Just tell us the spell, pumpkin."

And Jen leaned in and kissed Aoife's forehead.

But she did not wake, and she did not stir.

"Your parents, the not so grown up grownups, have taken you for granted, but it truly wasn't meant; it truly was not intended.

Is that why you left pumpkin?

Sometimes even when your eyes are open you cannot see that which matters; that which is right in front of you. Forgive us!

Deadlines and pressures have skewed our priorities. I say this by way of explanation and not to excuse adult misguidance. It is time for you, our beautiful girl, to step into safety. We will take the reins from here. Mummy and Daddy have opened their eyes and come home.

You are loved, so very loved. So much we did in the name of love and yet we forgot to include you, we weren't thinking outside the box. Security, safety and warmth, all of this you deserve, and a united front…" and Jen's voice trailed off as a lump emerged. She looked up and spotted Perry and blushed but continued. This time her eyes fixed upon his. "Wake up…Aubrey is waiting not too far away 120, 121, 122. Come out, come out wherever you are. Aoife, it's time." And Jen turned her head back towards her daughter. There was no change.

Perry swallowed, barely able to fight back the shame. *How did that saying go, 'love makes a home'* he thought. They had failed their children; he had failed to be a father, unable or unwilling to make the time in a season that both children love.

He looked at his daughter. *How long have you waited for a tree?* he pondered. *If nothing else, I should have made time for that.*

"Coffee," he said to Jen as she finished the sentence. And as Jen turned around, it seemed the words that she had narrated had also been evocative for her.

Jen stood up and wrapped her arms around Perry's neck as he held each coffee cup out to the sides and she kissed him and exited the room with her phone.

"No change. Aoife stable. Visiting hours 10:30 a.m. Big kiss to Aubrey. Love Jx", she pressed send. Jen then went to the ladies to freshen up and wash the sleep and the new and dried tears from her face.

15th December 07:00
Jeanne, Fred and Aubrey

Jeanne began texting back, *"Al well. Need to talk…"* then pressed delete, not wishing to create drama. She began again, *"All will. Aubrey haven't pancakes. Big kiss to Aoife and see u alter 10:30 a.m. Mx."*

Jeanne and Fred sat at the table with Aubrey. "Who wants to buy a Christmas tree?" Fred asked.

Jeanne looked at him and Aubrey shouted, "ME!"

Fred looked back at Jeanne and she smiled.

"Can you dig out the decorations and lights?" he asked.

"I think so, unless…well, unless they've been moved from their usual place," she stated.

"Good," Fred said and took a slurp of his freshly made coffee. "I'll drop you off at the hospital and go straight there. Don't tell the kids please," he asked, looking over his horn-rimmed glasses.

"Okay," Jeanne responded, excited by the prospect of feeling useful again but more so at the idea of joy filling this family home.

In truth, she knew that Jen and Perry would stop them so she had no intention of telling them of Fred's plans. They would do this for their grandchildren and although they may not appreciate it, it was important for Jen and Perry too, whatever was going on right now.

Fred washed the dishes and Jeanne let herself in to the study. In the corner was a cupboard made of rich, dark oak. She opened it and the bag of lights fell onto her feet. "You are keen to get out," she smiled picking them up. She then picked up the box resting on the bottom shelf and, with the bag resting on top, she carried the decorations to the living room.

"Aubrey," she said, approaching on her hands and knees where Aubrey was playing with his toys near the backdoor. "Aubrey."

He looked up with an expression that was both confused and excited, then his grandma continued, "I have a very important task for you. I need you to make sure Grandad buys the biggest tree that you see. Can you do that?"

Aubrey clapped, stood up and jumped. He clenched his fist then picked up Spark, throwing him up in the air and dropping him as he tried to catch him. Then from the top of his lungs, he shouted, "YAY!"

Fred and Jeanne laughed as Aubrey made himself dizzy running around in circles.

"We go now, Grandad?" he said, his jaw clenching tight as if he were about to burst.

"Soon, Aubrey," Fred replied, "when the clock says 9:30 a.m." Then he showed Aubrey where the big hand had to be and where the little one would sit when 9:30 o'clock comes on Grandad's watch.

Meanwhile, Fred sat as he untangled the lights ready for the tree while Jeanne made sandwiches and a flask of coffee with a hint of cinnamon and retrieved the rich tea biscuits from the suitcase, which she hadn't unpacked yet, placing them in a bag-for-life ready for the hospital visit.

Fred drove the car to the entrance and Jeanne leaned over to kiss Fred's cheek.

"You okay love, you're a bit early?" Fred asked.

"I don't have too long to wait and there's a cafeteria." Jeanne smiled. Then looking around at Aubrey she said, "The biggest tree, remember," and he beamed. He then picked up Spark and, with his arm outstretched, handed him to his grandma. Jeanne kissed it—not quite sure what else to do—and went to give it back, but Aubrey wouldn't take it.

"Spark will make Fifi better," he said in one clear sentence. And as Jeanne took it, she was so filled with love for her grandson she thought her heart would melt.

Fred didn't even turn around; he simply wiped the tear that had formed so quickly from that enormous gesture.

"Are you sure, Aubrey? I won't see you for a little while."

Aubrey simply said, "Fifi have Spark," and Jeanne left the car to the sound of an impatient horn from the vehicle behind them and carried her bag and Spark through the doors, aware of this significant milestone.

15th December 10:35
Jen, Perry and Jeanne

The doctor stood in the room. "Aoife's vital signs have improved and her temperature has risen, the irrigation appears to be working but, as you are well aware, Aoife is not awake so we need to keep monitoring and I'll be back this afternoon on my rounds, sooner if she wakes up."

"Is that possible? I mean, is it possible she may wake up in a couple of hours?" Jen asked.

"It is but, again, it is not guaranteed, but certainly we are in a much better place." Just at that moment, Jeanne walked through the door.

Perry waited for Aubrey to trail behind but only Jeanne entered, holding a carrier bag and Spark.

The doctor left and Jeanne placed herself next to her granddaughter's bed, her back to Jen and Perry. "Aoife, Aubrey has sent you a gift, he said it will make you better."

Perry and Jen looked at one another, their reaction mirroring one another. Jeanne tucked Spark under the blanket, resting it on Aoife's left arm, its head on her shoulder.

"Aubrey gave you Spark?" Perry asked, looking directly at Jeanne.

"Yep," Jeanne announced, "before I got out of the car. He said, 'Spark will make Aoife…I mean Fifi, better. Spark will make Fifi better.'"

"Well, I never," Perry said and a broad smile spread across his face. Jen smiled and, all at once, she felt so much love for this man and the family which was hers.

"I left Aubrey with your dad," Jeanne explained. "We weren't sure what was happening here so they will pick me, or perhaps you two, up in a few hours. I can sit here with Aoife for a while if you want to go home for a shower and a change of clothes," Jeanne continued.

"No, thank you, not with the possibility of Aoife waking up. We'll stay here," Perry responded, looking to Jen for confirmation.

"Yes, Aoife's temperature has gone up, they said the irrigation is working," Jen confirmed, adding a little more explanation.

"How did you sleep?" Jeanne asked.

"It was difficult, the nurses were in and out monitoring, making notes on the chart." Jen looked to the bottom of the bed where it sat.

"Were they?" Perry asked. "I didn't hear a thing."

Jeanne lifted the chart. 'Nil by mouth', she read, before skimming across the pages full of stats including the body temperature which finally rose at 7 a.m. to 36 degrees Celsius and then 36.5 by 10:25 a.m.

Jen watched her mother. It hadn't even occurred to her to check the notes and she felt foolish now. "36.5 degrees Celsius, what was it when she came in?" Jeanne asked.

"Just under 35, we were told," Perry responded.

"Sandwich?" Jeanne asked. Not really allowing for a yes or no response as she handed a brown paper bag each to Perry and Jen before pouring two cinnamon coffees. She was full on granary toast and coffee which she had drunk before leaving the house.

"How's Aubrey?" Jen asked, taking a bite from her sandwich.

"Oh gosh, how could I forget?" Jeanne said. Panic rose in both Perry and Jen. "Well, he sleepwalked into Aoife's bed and I slept their too. He takes up all of the room, you know…"

Both nodded.

"Anyway, I was woken at 2 a.m. by Aoife's alarm clock blasting out that…that superhero theme tune that she loves."

"2 a.m.?" Jen and Perry asked at once.

"Yes, it startled me," Jeanne confirmed.

"So that means…that means, if she set her alarm for 2 a.m., it's possible she left home sometime after?" Jen responded.

"She can set her alarm?" Perry asked. Nobody responded.

"Yes, that's what I believe," Jeanne confirmed. "As your dad says, we know the 'when' but not the 'why'."

"Only Aoife can tell us that," Perry answered while looking at his daughter, her tiny hand in his.

"Aubrey didn't stir," Jeanne said, responding to her daughter's earlier question. "He woke up refreshed and ate four pancakes, two pieces of apple, a slice of orange and drank a full bottle of water, then he played in the living room with his toys before they…" she was just about to give the secret away but checked herself, "before they dropped me here with Spark."

They all looked at the tatty, green dragon tucked under the blanket, consumed by their own thoughts knowing what a huge gesture that was from its small owner.

"It seems these past days have been life-changing in many ways," Jeanne said.

15th December Aoife

Aoife heard a rustling. She couldn't see or open her eyes no matter how much she tried. Her hands weren't so cold anymore and she tried to lift them to feel for Gingerbread, but she couldn't move a finger, a hand or an arm. She tried to speak but her mouth was shut tight and so she couldn't call her friend or anyone, so she lay still, listening to the rustling.

Through her shut eyelids, she could see light. *Had the sun come out*? she wondered.

No sooner she thought it, the dark descended and she disappeared again under its shadow and into nothing.

15th December 11:07
Fred and Aubrey

Aubrey excitedly watched as the man packed the tree into its string vest, as Grandad called it.

True to his word, Aubrey had picked the biggest and widest tree, which left Fred with a bit of a task trying to fit it into his car which was a foot shorter in length. Lucky for Fred, he wasn't short of a few bits and bobs in the back of his car and he was able to strap it in by bending its tip with a piece of rope he'd saved for…well, he had saved it for whenever he might need a piece of rope, so he guessed that was now.

Fred dragged it down the side of the house through the back gate, leaving it outside while he went back and, with Aubrey by his side, climbed the steps to the front door.

There were two boxes with Aoife's name sat at the front door. He picked them up and as he opened the door, a number of cards lay on the mat, all with Aoife's name on the envelopes.

Aubrey jumped over them, both feet together, and sat himself on the bench in the hall pulling off his wellingtons, coat and gloves, and raced to the backdoor with Grandad behind him holding the cards and packages.

Placing the mail on the table, Fred positioned the tree in the far corner of the living room where Jen and Perry usually erected it, and he set to work with Aubrey.

"Lights on first, then decorations," he said to his grandson.

Fred admitted to Aubrey, "It's good but not quite orderly. What do you think, will Aoife approve?"

Aubrey smiled, nodding his head. "Yes, yes, yes," he said, stamping his feet with glee before leaving his grandad to finish it while he watched cocooned on the red sofa.

With all but one decoration on the tree, Fred raised a hand to his grandson. "High-five," he said, and Aubrey hit him with all that he had. "Ah, ye have a strong arm there, me lad," he said in his worst pirate accent.

Fred then set the table for himself and took Aubrey to wash his hands and they both got stuck in to the ham sandwiches made by Grandma. Fred made himself a tea and Aubrey had apple juice, and they were in the car on their way to the hospital by 13:10.

At 13:45, an excited Aubrey and Fred walked through the door of Aoife's hospital room. Aubrey stood for a minute before approaching his daddy who lifted him up, saying, "Hey, pumpkin, look who's here," to a sleeping Aoife.

"She's not waking up?" Aubrey said, puzzlement across his face.

"No, not yet. She's still very tired," Perry said.

He sat Aubrey on the left side of the bed and removed his shoes. Aubrey turned to face Aoife. Lying on his left side, he picked up Spark to move closer to his sister. "Fifi, wake up. Fifi." He looked at his mummy. Jen didn't offer any words of hope, torn between wanting to comfort her son and not wanting to mislead him.

Aubrey leaned in further and whispered in Aoife's ear, "Fifi find the Christmas Spirit?"

Jen and Perry couldn't hear. "What did you say, munchkin?" Jen asked.

"It's a sprise," Aubrey said.

"What is?" Perry asked, a little more urgency in his voice.

Aubrey shook his head.

"It's okay, Aubrey. You're not in trouble, we're just wondering," Jen leaned forward and stroked his leg, squeezing it gently while smiling at him.

Aubrey didn't offer anything but Jeanne said, "He said that to me yesterday…Aoife got a surprise? I didn't really understand what he meant and then I forgot about it with all that has been going on."

With all eyes on Aubrey, he looked worried. "Tell me about Aoife's surprise," Fred asked. "Was it an ice cream?"

Aubrey shook his head, smiling, "Nooo."

"Was it a…biscuit?"

"Nooo," he said again.

"Okay, I give up, what was it?" Fred said, pulling a face and raising his hands in defeat.

Aubrey looked at Aoife. "Fifi was finding the Christmas Spirit," he said, pronouncing Christmas Spirit as slowly and precisely as his big sister had and looking around at all four adults whose gazes were fixated on him.

"The Christmas Spirit?" Perry asked. Aubrey nodded.

"Did Aoife say anything else, Aubrey?" Jen asked softly.

"Ummm," he nodded.

"It's okay, Aubrey, what did she say?" Jen continued.

"Fifi went to the North Ball to see Father Christmas. It's a surprise for Mummy."

Jen thought for a minute and repeated, "The North Pole to see Father Christmas for me?"

Aubrey nodded.

"Did she say why?" Jen continued.

Aubrey looked at his mother with that look that to Jen said, 'I'm watching for signs, a twitch, a frown could blow it now,' and so she sat, her eyes smiling as broadly as her lips and she squeezed his leg once more to reassure him that all will be well.

"Uhhh, Fifi, she asking Father Christmas to find the Christmas Spirit to make Mummy happy." And again, Aubrey was careful to pronounce Christmas Spirit just the way Aoife had.

As the words sunk in, Jen lifted her hand to her mouth and inhaled. Aubrey looked at Perry.

"Thank you, Aubrey," he said, "You've been a very good boy." Perry leaned in and gave him a hug while Jen sunk in to her chair under the weight of Aubrey's words.

15th December
Aoife and the Voice

"Aoife, Aoife," the voice spoke softly.

I can't speak, she thought as she tried to move her lips.

"I can hear you," the voice said.

"You can?" Aoife asked. "But my mouth isn't moving."

"Nevertheless, I can," it replied.

"Where are you?" Aoife asked.

"Here, there, all around," the voice came back. "Within you, without you, everywhere," it chuckled.

"Where am I?" Aoife responded.

"You? You're nowhere," the voice said and it laughed some more.

"That's not funny! I must be somewhere," she protested.

"Nope, you are nowhere at all, not up, not down, not all around, just nowhere," the voice mocked.

"Why can't I open my eyes?" Aoife asked after a pause.

"You can," it responded.

Aoife tried with all of her might but her eyes wouldn't open. "I can't," she said, "I just tried."

"You can if you choose, if you decide," the voice said.

"I do choose," she said.

"What do you choose?" it asked.

"I choose to open my eyes!" Aoife said.

"No, that's not it, you need to choose," the voice repeated.

Aoife swallowed the sadness. "I don't know what you mean." She tried lifting a finger but it didn't move. It was as if it weighed too much.

The voice laughed. "Nope, that won't do it."

"Why are you laughing at me?" Aoife asked.

"Because you're silly," the voice came back.

"I'm not!" Aoife protested.

"Oh yes, you are!" the voice said.

"Oh no…" and Aoife didn't join in the pantomime, she wasn't in the mood.

"Well, you can't be that smart or you wouldn't be stuck nowhere in the nothing. You're the one that got yourself here. There's nobody else to blame," it said, this time no frivolity in its voice. "Fact!"

"What do you see?" it asked Aoife.

"I don't see anything, my eyes are shut," Aoife responded.

"Like I said, silly! You don't need eyes to see," it said, yawning as if she were boring it.

"I don't…" Aoife didn't complete. "I see snow and trees and Gingerbread."

"Nope, that's where you have been, what do you see? Look harder and deeper." After some deliberation, images popped in to Aoife's head. "I see Mummy, she's wearing her hair in a bun with her glasses on the tip of her nose and she's writing, but when I come in, she looks at me and smiles with her eyes and her lips curling up. She's pleased to see me. Mummy stops writing and holds me tight, so very tight that I think I might not breathe. I see Daddy, he's home before the clock says seven and he watches 'In the Night Garden' and he holds me tight so that I might not breathe if he doesn't let me go from his squeeze. I see Aubrey jumping up with more excitement than he can possibly manage, and he races towards me and knocks me off my feet so that I fall back on to the sofa, the big red sofa, and he laughs like Aubrey laughs and I can't help but join in, and it never matters why we laugh, he just makes me do it."

"What do you feel?" the voice asked.

This time, the thing in her throat that she usually swallowed to stop the tears filled her up with something else. "Love," she said. "I feel love."

"Okay," the voice said. "What will you do now?" it continued.

"I'm going home," Aoife said and paused before she left. "Who are you?" Aoife asked.

"If you listen and really hear, you already know the answer, silly," the voice said and then fell into the silence.

15th December 14:30
Jen and Aoife

Jen sat in the room alone. Perry had gone for some fresh air and to raid the cafeteria while Jeanne and Fred had taken Aubrey for a play in the family room. But Spark was firmly in place in Aoife's embrace.

Jen bent over to kiss Aoife on the cheek and puff the pillow on which she lay.

Aoife smelt the familiar essence of home as the cinnamon scent encompassed her.

Picking up 'A Christmas Carol' Jen read on.

This story was so familiar to them all. It almost felt as though Jen could recite each line verbatim. A story that showed that habits of old, those which no longer serve you well, are best left behind. We all have a choice: dwell on an imperfect, unkind past or learn from it and make good instead. It is a wonderful gift to be able to see, when once the path chosen by you was shrouded in darkness; blinded by hate. It is a story that speaks of a future filled with kindness and love towards humankind because of spirits that afforded an individual deep reflection and future insight. The story shows, in vivid colour and descriptive pros, how our actions could make or break another. Therefore, to what end would you choose destruction and power? The difference between despair and hope is living not merely existing.

Perry and Jen had forgotten to be grateful for what they have; their bank of knowledge overshadowed by misguided actions and striving. This year a wake-up call reminded them all, family is invaluable; worth more than titles and gold. Jen pondered this between the paragraphs as she stared at her daughter.

Aoife heard the familiar voice, it made her heart race and a lump grew in her throat, yet still her eyes were firmly shut.

Jen looked up, placed the book on her lap. She looked at her daughter: a tear drop, water upon her cheek. Jen looked up to the ceiling in case it had leaked, looking for evidence and surety. "Aoife, Aoife."

Aoife thought the calling of her name had never felt so comforting and although the tears escaped, her eyes didn't open and, try as she might, her fingers wouldn't move, her hands were pressed like heavy weights on nothing yet something solid and soft all at once, and her arms wouldn't move to her mind's will and her tears rolled.

Jen stood over Aoife and, leaning closer, whispered in her ear, "Pumpkin, it's okay, don't be afraid, you can wake up now. Come home."

"I want to," Aoife said but her lips remained tightly shut.

"What will you choose?" the voice had gone but the words circulated around and around in her mind.

"I choose to go home! I will go home." And all at once, she bent a finger with her will.

Jen laughed and cried and said, "That's it, Aoife, that's it, it's time." And Jen's tears dropped onto Aoife's face, flowing in a beautiful embrace with her own.

Aoife's hand lifted, had she grown strong or had the weight fallen off? Jen placed Aoife's hand in hers. "Come on, Aoife, you're almost here. We've been waiting for you to wake up."

Aoife willed her mind to tell her body to yield to its command and her eyelids fluttered, not quite unstuck. She rested then tried calling upon her entire might.

"Aoife. You've got this, my clever pumpkin," Jen said, the tears streaming and her eyes beaming all at once.

Aoife's eyes were open just like that and for a moment, the words were unspoken as mother and daughter locked in, fixed as if seeing each other for the very first time.

"Hello, my beautiful, beautiful girl. We've missed you."

"Hello, Mummy," Aoife said, and Jen pressed the buzzer then kneeled down beside her daughter, clasping her hand and stroking her auburn hair.

"Look," Jen said as she leaned over and held up the green, tatty dragon.

Aoife, weak from her ordeal, smiled through teary eyes as her mother tucked Spark back into its place.

17th December 16:35
The Christmas Spirit

Aoife stared out of the car window at the Christmas lights. They twinkled, white, blue, red and some had all the colours of the rainbow. Some houses were garishly decorated with Father Christmas and 'Santa Stop Here' signs while reindeer or snowmen or both stood on garden lawns with dignity and splendour.

Front facades were adorned with enough fairy lights to light up the town, on more than one house, while others had stickers or snow upon their windows. In the middle of the square, the angel was bright, strung up high between the lamp-posts and its gaze seemed to follow her. Stars lit the way to the church and all around the square and up the path towards the church, a manger with donkeys and a crib lit up in yellowed glory.

Aoife's head drooped, she'd caused so much trouble already she wondered if it was appropriate to ask Daddy to get the tree with only seven days until Christmas Eve.

Jen was watching in the mirror as her daughter drank it in, and as Aoife slumped against the window, she didn't offer a word to her daughter as she knew what she was thinking.

Jen took out her phone as they pulled onto their drive. 'NOW', she sent, and all at once, 34 Burgundy Road burst into light. White and blue twinkled around the doors and windows and sparkled on the shrubs dotted across the small patch of lawn. Aoife and Aubrey sat in the car mesmerised then watched on as the drive lit up like a runway bordering the green to guide them in. Aoife laughed out loud, she couldn't help herself, and Aubrey joined in. Spark sat strapped in between them, his duty done.

Fred and Jeanne stood on the steps of the door watching their family mount the stairs, Aoife holding on to the side and on to her mother as she soaked up the scene before her.

"Me lady," Fred said. Through the door, more surprises await Aoife.

"Cinnamon!" she said, removing shoes and coat. There on the table was a feast of tea, cakes and a plate of rich tea biscuits with a sign that said, 'AOIFE'S. DO NOT TOUCH!'

It was all too much for Aoife to take in. Perry picked up a tie and folded it across her eyes, saying, "One more thing, pumpkin, and the pièce de résistance of changes at number 34."

Unable to see—well, she had to admit the light did stream from the floor—but unable to see ahead, she allowed herself to be guided and it was Aubrey's excitement that made her heart pound in anticipation.

"Ready?" Perry asked. Aoife nodded, not quite sure.

And as the tie came off, she stood in front of the most magnificent tree she had ever seen and it was here in her living room, lit up with lights that worked, blue and white, and she wasn't quite sure why, but she sat down folding her legs and simply scanned the tree.

There on the bottom was her decoration, the one she made when she was four: it was a star but equally barely one at all. She looked around to her mummy, Jen nodded in their unspoken exchange. And there, a little higher, was Aubrey's. Well, she wasn't quite sure what the red crepe paper was but they'd decided a long time ago that it was Father Christmas.

She thought about her journey the past three days: her meeting with Father Christmas, her ride upon the reindeer and her walk with Gingerbread.

Her head drooped at missing her friend, at having missed her play and also at having failed on her mission to find the Christmas Spirit.

"One more thing, pumpkin, can you see what's missing?" From where she sat, Aoife couldn't and so she stood up and looked at the tree so magnificent, her gaze moving its way up its splendour.

Perry pulled his hand from behind his back and, looking at Aoife, said, "Are you ready?"

"Yes," she said, the tickling in her belly had already started.

"Climb on, it's time to finish it off," Perry said as he kneeled on the floor.

Aoife placed both legs over her daddy's shoulder and reached and stretched, careful not to pull her stitches. It was almost too high for her to reach. But when she had finished, the star sat upon its top then the audience gave a round of applause and Aoife sat on her daddy's shoulders, marvelling for a moment.

Jen followed her mother into the kitchen. "I didn't mean…"

"Well, daughter of mine, you did say make tea…and what do you see before you?"

She wanted to say, 'a plethora of sugary over stimulation,' but she said, "Love with a hint of deliberate misinterpretation," as she smiled at her mother and hugged her close.

Perry, Fred and Jeanne busied themselves in the kitchen as Jen sat on the red sofa listening to her daughter's adventures about her ride on the deer, her visit to the workshop, the hot chocolate Peggy Christmas made, about Gingerbread and Stick, about the elf and the storm that blew them off on their way home and how she was lost and couldn't find her way.

Jen listened to all of it and then asked, "What made you go in search for the Christmas Spirit?"

By this time, Perry had joined them and was sat on the arm of the sofa. Aoife looked to him and her mummy and said, "I heard you, you and Daddy were being cross and you said you couldn't find it."

Jens hands clasped her mouth and Perry looked at his wife. "Oh, Aoife, I'm so sorry."

"We're sorry," Perry said.

When she had composed herself, Jen looked at Aoife. "Aoife, the Christmas Spirit I referred to has no form: it has no gender, it is neither a person, an animal, an insect nor anything that you can put your finger on; it is something that is within you. It is an emotion."

And she paused, looking around the room as she formulated her words. "The Christmas Spirit is something that comes from within you and it is, I see now, one of the biggest gifts of all. It is not selfish, it is not valuable, but it is giving and invaluable—priceless, in fact. Does that make sense?"

"I think so but..." Aoife responded.

"Let me try," Perry said. "The Christmas Spirit is all of this," he said, his arms sweeping the house, "it is in the baking, the water, the tea and even the offering of a biscuit like your rich tea," he said tickling her gently. "And it is in the cooking of the feast and it is in the decorating of the tree and it lives within you and me, your mummy, your grandparents and in everybody who celebrates this time of year."

"The gifts," Perry continued and Aoife couldn't help notice many boxes and cards beneath the tree as her gaze was averted by her daddy's words. "They are part of the giving. I suppose a gesture of love, a one-time opportunity to show rather than tell," Perry said, looking at his wife.

Jen was all too aware that she hadn't yet addressed the reason that Aoife left to make things better. "Aoife, I think it's time we explain and please don't worry if you don't understand it all."

Aoife nodded, not really sure what was coming but a knot was forming in her stomach.

"Daddy and Mummy have been unhappy and we're sorry that this has affected you so deeply. Our actions should never be your responsibility." Perry stroked Aoife's hair. Aoife sat, her eyes locked in to her mummy's. "You being missing was the saddest and most frightening thing that your daddy and I, and your grandparents and Aubrey, and your friends and teachers have had to endure, and it made us wake up from the bubble we were in."

Aoife couldn't help visualising her mummy and daddy in a bubble floating up to the sky, worried that it may pop and they'd come crashing down. She banished the picture in her mind.

"Well, that bubble has burst and Daddy and I have some work to do but your actions…and before I say this, please never ever, ever leave us like that again," and she smiled so Aoife, seeing it in her eyes, smiled too, "your action did bring the Christmas Spirit home."

"It did?" she asked.

"Yes, pumpkin, it did," Jen responded, squeezing Aoife's hand.

"Is there anything else you'd like to know, pumpkin?" Daddy asked.

Aoife didn't have to think too long. "Will I ever see Gingerbread again? I really miss him."

"About that…" Perry smiled. "Gingerbread's real name is, in fact, Toby, and maybe, possibly, but you need to rest now. Remember what the doctor said." He winked.

Aoife chuckled at the idea that Gingerbread was in fact Toby. *Toby didn't suit him at all,* she thought silently. Then she closed her eyes, crossed her fingers and made a wish. Jen and Perry simply looked at one another and then the clock.

17th December 18:30
The Reunion

Jeanne and Fred had just finished putting the last dish in the cupboard when the doorbell rang. Aoife lay on the red sofa, her unicorn blanket covering her and her eyes almost shut. "Come on in," she heard her grandma say and then she heard a familiar ringing of a bell. It took but a moment for Aoife to sit up and as her head popped over the arm of the chair a red, coarse haired dog came bounding towards her.

"Gingerbread!" she shouted, the word stretching out across the room and the dog, as pleased to see her, jumped up onto the arm of the chair and head-butted Aoife.

Aoife laughed and cried all at once as she rubbed her head with her hand and Toby licked her tears before jumping on the sofa and cuddling in to her.

"Ow," Aoife said, a little bruised from her catheter and cannula but she held him close nevertheless.

"Bring him back when you're ready. I'm in all day and me address is in the bag," Geoff, his owner, said extending his hand, holding the canvas bag containing food and treats. Perry thanked him as they shook hands. "I'm so glad you found her," Geoff said, turning to leave. At the bottom of the steps, he said, "He'll need to go for a walk before bed, you don't want…well, you know," and with that, he waved and continued on his way.

Perry watched until Geoff was out of sight. He looked up at the stars then closed his eyes and inhaled a breath that filled him up. It was as if it were his first for a while. Shutting the door, he returned to the cacophony of smells and the hearth of his family.

Aoife fell asleep and Toby stayed beside her, not getting up to eat or drink and not caring for the outdoors either.

He simply lay guard. When Perry carried Aoife to bed, Toby followed in an uncompromising strut and took his position at the bottom of her bed.

24th December 20:00
Christmas Eve

Aoife sat for a long time looking up at the sky. The moon was a Waxing Gibbous and the North Star, so reliable, was where it always was.

As she had each night, she thanked them for their guide and there she sat, the clock slowly pushing on with its digital minutes and she waited and waited.

She thought she must have slept for a moment, even though she'd stretched her eyelids open whenever they got heavy, because all of a sudden, the time had jumped from 21:03 to 23:45. "Almost time," she said.

She heard the jingling first. *Unmistakably reindeer,* she thought, excitement whirling within and her cheeks ached because her mouth wouldn't stop grinning.

"Ho, ho, ho."

There it was: the sleigh, the reindeer and, in his red suit, Father Christmas.

She expected him to fly across the moon and she would wave and say her thank you. But he was flying directly towards her.

Father Christmas stopped right outside her window, perfectly still with a little jolting from the deer but they hovered, sat in mid-air.

"Wow," was about all Aoife could say.

"Hello, Aoife," Father Christmas said. Standing up, she leaned towards him as far as she could and, stretching out her arms, she placed both of her hands on his cheeks, his beard soft underneath her touch. "Thank you," she said.

"Oh, Aoife, it wasn't me," said Father Christmas and winked. "You brought the Christmas Spirit home. Remember, whenever you feel that you or anybody you love is without, look within."

Aoife nodded and focused on the magnificent stag who had taken her to the North Pole and almost back. He hung his head as if not wanting to meet her gaze.

"Hello…" Aoife said staring directly at him. He lifted his head just a little and looked in her direction. "I don't blame you. Thank you, I loved our ride."

The deer nodded and tapped his hoof upon the invisible surface.

"Merry Christmas, Aoife," Father Christmas said and he lifted his reins, shouting, "Onwards my magnificent friends! We have much to do tonight! Merry Christmas, dearest Aoife!" The words were already distant and trailing off as the sleigh moved on at lightning speed.

"Merry Christmas," Aoife shouted and she lay down thinking of the two questions she had intended to ask, but had not; she had simply forgotten to remember. Yawning, she mulled her questions over. *Why is Father Christmas also known as Santa or St Nicholas? No that's not right at all,* she thought. *There are so many more names and in so many different languages.* Her head was spinning at the birth of yet more questions. *How many names, in how many languages?* she wondered. She took a deep breath then yawned again and decided she would consult her encyclopaedia or the internet another day. As her eyes shut she concentrated on the one question only. *Which reindeer did I ride on?*

With sleep pulling her into its embrace she thought of the speed at which the reindeer had travelled. Then all at once she smiled because she realised she knew the answer. With that conundrum solved Aoife let go of her busy thoughts and slept.

The End